THE CATTLE CAR

GEORGES HYVERNAUD

THE CATTLE CAR

Including LETTER TO A LITTLE GIRL

With an Afterword by Roland Desné

Translated by Dominic Di Bernardi and
Austryn Wainhouse

THE MARLBORO PRESS/NORTHWESTERN

EVANSTON, ILLINOIS

The Marlboro Press/Northwestern
Northwestern University Press
Evanston, Illinois 60208-4210

Originally published in French under the title *Le Wagon à vaches.*
Copyright © 1985 by Editions Ramsay, Paris. English translation
copyright © 1997 by Dominic Di Bernardi. "Letter to a Little Girl"
originally published in French under the title "Lettre à une petite fille," in
Georges Hyvernaud, *Lettre anonyme, nouvelles et autres inédits;*
copyright © 1986 by Editions Ramsay, Paris. Published by permission of
Andrée Hyvernaud. English translation copyright © 1997 by Austryn
Wainhouse. Afterword by Roland Desné published by permission of
Roland Desné. English translation copyright © 1997 by Austryn
Wainhouse. Published 1997 by The Marlboro Press/Northwestern.

The publication of this volume has been made possible in part by a grant
from the National Endowment for the Arts.

ISBN 0-8101-6030-7 (cloth)
ISBN 0-8101-6031-5 (paper)

Library of Congress Cataloging-in-Publication Data

Hyvernaud, Georges.
  [Wagon à vaches. English]
  The cattle car ; including, Letter to a little girl / Georges
Hyvernaud ; with an afterword by Roland Desné; translated by
Dominic Di Bernardi and Austryn Wainhouse.
    p. cm.
  ISBN 0-8101-6030-7 (cloth : alk. paper). — ISBN 0-8101-
6031-5 (pbk. : alk. paper)
  I. Di Bernardi, Dominic. II. Wainhouse, Austryn. III. Title.
PQ2615.Y8W313 1997
843'.914—dc21   97-2987
                                                      CIP

The paper used in this publication meets the minimum
requirements of the American National Standard for Information
Sciences—Permanence of Paper for Printed Library Materials,
ANSI Z39.48-1984.

CONTENTS

LETTER TO A LITTLE GIRL

At the time of my last leave—it will soon be five years ago—you were a tiny little creature toddling about on the sand, full of wonder before the seashells and pebbles. True, seashells and pebbles are wondrous things. But having seen them for so long, we older ones are unable to see them anymore. It takes a child's wonder to make us discover them. Children are constantly teaching grown-ups . . .

Then down over that brief moment of light came five heavy years, and this absence, and this anguish. Between us were laid down inhuman layers of events and geographies. And now you are this unknown little girl inhabited by memories, by friendships, by tales, by songs I do not know. This little girl, this little stranger: my daughter . . . And I am an unhappy man. A sort of hobo, worse than a hobo. I am writing to you in a barn where it is dark and cold. In here we are several hundred captive men, crowded together, guarded, threatened and insulted at every turn. During the whole of today we have had just about nothing to eat. It has been a long time since we last washed ourselves. We have almost no more underclothes or shoes. I am writing to you so that later on you will know that this destituteness and this humiliation were my lot—later on, when I myself shall have forgotten. For one does forget.

Not that I ask you to pity me. Above all not that. It is proper that at least once in his life each one really experience the world's cruelty. That he touch bottom. It is a right that one has, the right to know how hard it is, how difficult and dangerous, to conduct the human adventure. Those who must be pitied are those who are protected from everything, who elude everything—the men with gloved hands.

When at nightfall I lie down in my beggardom, overcome with hunger and weariness, shivering beneath my filthy blanket, and most fortunate indeed to have a blanket, I say to myself that this, this is mankind's true situation. And this is to know it as it must be known; not by way of the brain, not by way of philosophies, but in one's dead-tired flesh. Then one understands. One understands that ten-story houses, telephones and refrigerators, and the policeman at the intersection, all that is mere appearance. Appearance, too, is the book under the lighted lamp, and the friends around the table; appearance, the stabilities and the securities. But hunger, servitude, fever, flight—that's what's true, that's what's durable. The constants, the permanent features of our human fate.

For weeks we have been struggling across unending plains, in snow, under falling snow, in slush and in mud, without knowing where we are being led or whether this will ever end. In villages lying outside of time, men and women, with expressions of animal stupor, watch us pass. Poles, Ukrainians, Serbs—how is one to tell? Wrapped up in rags the color of dirt and of stone walls. All slaves. You are reminded of those medieval peasants history books talk about. And on the roads, in everlasting lines come inexhaustibly, from Posen, from Bromberg, the refugees' slow-moving, rickety wagons, covered by hideous multicolored carpets, led by hunched-over old men, shaggy under their now hairless fur hats. People who were given the order to leave for the West, and they left, and that is all they know about it. And that, too, is out of the Middle Ages, out of the times of great fear and of exodus. We have not yet got out of the Middle Ages, despite our cities and books and all the things we believe. We are still in the year 1000.

I have thought about these things while trudging along the roads. Although it can hardly be called thinking when with each step the whole body is racked by a suffering beyond which it seems there can be nothing further to do but die. It takes hold of you in the knees, in the shoulders, in the thighs, everywhere. And it burns you, it bites right into you. And there are your infected frostbitten feet. And there are your intestines wrung by dysentery. You cough. You moan. You are nothing but a heap of sickness and pain. And so merely to take one step becomes a terrifying problem. To pick your foot up once again and to put it down a little ahead. To succeed one more time in wrenching your foot from the snow and in swinging it forward. Just to do that. Tiny victory, lasting only an instant, but which demands so much will. So much artfulness, for there are ways of fooling this dead-tired body. By going about it properly, by calculating carefully, you manage to economize ever so slightly on effort, to reduce your suffering by that much.

When a man is at that point—at the end of his tether, as they say, his strength all gone, his hope all gone—when a man is at that point he does not think a great deal. Nevertheless, one is forced to conclude that the mill never stops grinding out its ideas. Even in moments of extreme distress ideas still keep occurring to you. To be sure, they are poor ideas. The ideas a poor man would have. So simple as to be pitiable. Not those pretty ideas that enable you to stand out. Not those ideas that are like toys. No; rough-hewn and plodding ideas. Play with ideas; I, too, did a bit of that. In the past. It's not so very difficult: the whole trick is to go about it as if reality did not exist. But when you are right in the middle of it, you stop saying all but two or three very commonplace things to yourself. Two or three things that really count. Obvious, essential things. Born of an experience altogether devoid of sham. Human things. The rest—it's for the chimpanzees at play in drawing rooms and in academic wonderlands.

You ask yourself what you are doing here and why you are doing it, why you are holding on, how you are holding on.

Astonishment at these resources you were not aware you possessed. Never would I have believed I was capable of carrying any such load. This body which is no longer youthful and which is being put out of order in so many places, I knew nothing of its capacity to resist as marvelously as it has done. There is nothing like being tested by events. I am measuring this body of mine—this adversary, this friend. I am discovering the hurt I can fear from it, but I am also experiencing its fidelity. And if I speak of the body, it is from a kind of modesty. There is indeed something else besides my body. There is me. And there is this: that I can rely upon myself far more than I had hoped.

In the eyes of the Germans the whole thing is very clear. The Germans have placed sentinels with guns and dogs on our flanks. When one of us no longer has the strength to advance, the sentinels set a dog on him. Or else threaten to shoot him. Wherewith, strength or no strength, he is prevailed upon to advance. The sentinels' art of persuasion, you have it there in a nutshell. And in a sense one must not scorn these keepers of men for their pessimism. It is undeniably effective. Fear is also a factor. But the jailer's viewpoint does not explain everything. Does not explain much at all. For a moment comes when it is no longer his fear of a bullet that a man has to overcome, but his desiring a bullet. A moment when it would be so simple to lie down in the snow and await the shot. To be done with it, done with this whole world of snow and guns . . .

You wonder why you keep on. "Because I am not alone," I was told by one of my companions who is a believer. Another, who does not believe in the same gods (although perhaps they are the same), recalled a passage in a book. And yet books do not weigh heavy in these dire situations. The majority of books. Out of all those pages that one has read, out of all those words, how many are there that may help one to live when life becomes an evil for man? But, it may be added, there is no surer way to evaluate the quality of a work. It's something other than the decidings of a critic who writes in the newspapers. When a sentence from a book comes looking for you in your dark night and comes bringing you succor, then there can be no mistake about it: the sign of greatness is upon that book. All grave experiences simplify things, we recognize that simplification here. The authentic separates from the parody. We find we have forgotten everything, nearly everything, except for a few words. It's that none of the rest deserved any better. Clevernesses without importance, hollow fineries. Misfortune acts upon them like an acid. Only some hard, incorrodible prominences remain.

To wit, that page from Saint-Exupéry from which my companion was quoting. The sentinels had allowed us a ten-minute rest. Everyone dropped his bundle and sank to the ground. Men lay scattered about, pell-mell, like empty sacks. Their faces, the faces of chain-gang convicts, brutalized, sullen, unshaven. It was then, as he sat cautiously rubbing his swollen knee, that a boy next to me repeated what Guillaumet said to Saint-Exupéry after having made his way through unspeakable peril: "What I did there, I swear no animal would have done." One of those decisive remarks that illuminates everything. You wonder why you keep on. Because I am not alone, says one. And the other—and it could be the same person: because man is a creature that does not give up. You keep on, without any purpose, for nothing, you just do it, because you are a man.

We are not always proud of our species. Occasions do not lack for despising men. Especially men who are hungry: hunger does not embellish them. I have seen some who would rob their comrades of the small amount of bread and soup they give us. You come to believe that dignity and decency are virtues for the use of well-fed people only, and that they do not stand up before a certain misery. Acrid maxims, which we derive I know not what satisfaction from formulating. There is a temptation, it does seem, to content oneself with this summary misanthropy, to take pleasure in it. But one must avoid judgments of this sort. Not that they are false; they are neither true nor false. We should not expect too much of others. In the world of war, one is alone. Shut up within one's own drama, attentive solely to oneself. He will be severely rebuffed who opens and offers himself to everyone, and seeks for kindness about him. Do not expect too much of others, but do not expect too little either. That man capable of stealing a piece of bread is just as capable of giving his last piece of bread away. Human beings are like that, a mixture of good and bad. Like the sky, from which we have sunshine and rain, smiles and furies. And however it all adds up, one has to believe in man even so.

Believe in man and believe in life: life is like man and like the sky. Even in those hours when everything seems to be receding from us, to life there still remains that wherewith the heart rejoices. There remain those elementary treasures of whose value we have no inkling when we are entirely happy. I would like to tell you of the simple riches, water and bread, and the straw in barns—the thick and helpful straw where one lies down and stretches out and that, underneath your weight, makes its soft rustling sound of silk and rain. Bread, water . . . I have gone up to old people standing in their doorways to beg water from them, and been driven back by blows from the sentinels' rifle butts. That seems more precious than anything else in the world, water you have desired for hours on end and that you drink at last, in haste, from a rusty tin can. They who have never had to do anything but turn a tap to have all the water they want do not know an important secret.

When a man lists to himself the things existence has taught him, he finds he is quickly done. And the things he enumerates are never very subtle nor very profound. But what he arrives at is at least his. He has bought and paid for it with his sweat and blood. He has not borrowed it. He is not parroting something others have told him. He can make a gift of it to his child.

I give you these pages written with a pencil in a soiled little notebook at the end of a hard day. They are not, I know, right for your age. Though the tragedies of our time have done violence to every soul, yet they are powerless against childhood's dreams. You are not quite eight years old. You are a little girl who goes to school with a ribbon in her hair. In your mind take place dazzling colloquies between wild beasts and flowers. The animals in your fables protect you from our catastrophic dramas. And that is why I wanted to gather together for you these teachings of a bitter experience. Because the inflexible unknowing of a child freezes the lie upon a grown man's lips. Because any temptation to fix up, to falsify what we know about reality is confounded by the mere thought of the look that lights the face of a little girl of eight.

THE CATTLE CAR

I don't choose my friends.

—STENDHAL

Bourladou often asks me: "So tell me, what the hell would you be up to, all by yourself that way, in your room like that, night after night?"

Because the moment he, Bourladou, isn't talking to someone, he's dying of boredom.

Whatever the hell I might be up to is none of Bourladou's business. Or anybody else's. I'm eating away at it, hollowing out a hole for myself. You're not going to tell me a man hasn't the right to eat away at it and hollow out a hole for himself.

"I read, you know, I work . . . "

"Oh yeah," Bourladou goes. "Right."

Eat away at it, hollow out a hole for yourself inside the thickness of the city and the density of the night. And scrunch down inside there, scratching yourself, licking yourself, while waiting for sleep and death.

Bourladou looks at the books scattered on my table, and wonders just what it could be, this work of mine.

"If only you had the radio to listen to," he says.

No need for a radio. All you need do is sit on your bed. And stay there. Listening to the stubborn little noise that life makes.

I have put in my eight hours over at Busson Brothers, Sparkling Water. Now I'm sitting on my bed. Look at me. Sitting between four shabby red-papered walls. Behind the walls, there are other living souls. Half-alive. Dead tired and limp, like me. There's the Crazy Lady and the Old Folks. There's Iseult. I'm getting some faint gurglings of voices, the distant knock of a pitcher hitting a basin . . .

Iseult: that's Bourladou's nickname for that tall girl, lean and bitter. She's a clerk in a hardware store. Bourladou, when in his lewd humor, pretends to believe Iseult and I sleep together.

"Hats off to you, you old rooster, you must be having a time of it with that little chick."

I contrive some subtle laughter.

"Hot-blooded, that woman," Bourladou says, "it's obvious. She's got curves, pizzazz, real sex appeal."

Every Saturday Iseult goes out on some sort of camping trip or other. I run into her on the stairs, bowed down under the grotesque pack on her back. Twenty pounds of hiking boots on her feet. Scrawny, sunburned legs stick out of a pair of Boy Scout shorts. That's Iseult. Thirty hours of camping and the rest of the week in her hardware store. And the same thing from week to week. A tidy little destiny, no loose ends. The destiny of an insect, along the lines of mine and lots of others. Destiny, indeed: the word is rather excessive for the designating of this bleak assent to existence.

The two Old Folks must be having a quarrel. She's taking him to task over his cigarettes. Forty-five francs a pack. Everybody can see it's not you who's bringing home the money.

"I only smoked two," the Old Guy says.

"That makes two too many," the Old Lady says.

Walls, and people between walls, with their disputes, their fatigue, that day's-end bitterness, that disgust.

Bourladou has taken off that handsome shaggy jacket of his. Removed his watch, his eyeglasses. Removed his false teeth. Perhaps right now he is talking about me to Madame Bourladou, perhaps he is telling her that I'm really a lost soul. Madame Bourladou is spreading cream over her acne rosacea. She's answering, I hope, that I do look that way, but underneath I'm really . . .

"A very cultivated young fellow, I assure you. He reads all sorts of stuff."

"Nah, nah," says Bourladou. He's in his undershorts. He moves about. A species of monstrous fowl. He scratches his buttocks. He is reminded that he is putting on weight, that he ought to get back to daily exercising.

"We could invite him over one of these evenings," says Madame Bourladou.

"Invite who?" Bourladou asks. "Oh, right. My mind was somewhere else. Sure we could."

He spreads his legs, tries to touch his left foot with his right hand, his right foot with his left hand. Excellent exercise for the abdominals. Madame Bourladou, in her nightgown (pale pink), gazes at him: "You're mad. Right after your meal."

"I'm out of shape," Bourladou sighs, straightening up.

He is going to go to bed. They are all going to go to bed. And the dentures are going to go to bed in the glasses of water, the eyeglasses in their little black cases, the watches upon the night tables. This is the moment when humankind comes undone, disperses, falls into scattered pieces, gives up the coherent appearances it assumes sixteen hours a day. The hour of truth. All that we kept so carefully together, the real teeth and the false teeth, the real hearts and the false hearts, the false collars and the real necks, the widows and the widows' weeds, the legs and the nylon stockings, it all comes loose, unties, separates. Pretty amusing to imagine. My compatriots snuggled up in their beds, and all around the elements of their propriety and their importance. Only the backs of chairs are now wearing jackets. And only the jackets are wearing decorations . . .

My colleague Porcher is going to go to bed. In the kitchen decked with diapers drying above the stove, his day comes to an end in sounds of water, in children's tears and evening prayers.

The latest born has been asleep for a while: he's six months old, nothing much to be said about him. The oldest kid is reciting his lesson on the metric system. Porcher monitors the multiples and submultiples of the gram. At the same time he battles against his sore throat with steaming hot water and yellow tablets. Hunched over, face buried in an enameled stewpot, he's halfway scalded but he is holding on. You have to show the children you've got character.

"Mimile," Madame Porcher asks, "you did pull the garden gate all the way shut, didn't you?"

Madame Porcher, for her part, is trying to remove the clothes from a howling Loulou. All the day's-end concerns are assailing her at the same time. Madeleine, did you remember to do pipi? Emile, you didn't forget to wind the clock?

"Wmmm," replies Porcher from the depths of his inhaler.

From the adjoining room comes Madeleine's dutiful voice: "Who art in Heaven, give us this day . . . "

"The decagram," Jean-Paul recites.

"Give us this day," Madeleine drones, "this day . . . "

"The hectogram," Jean-Paul says. "The kilometer."

"Wmmm," from Porcher, who has raised and is sternly agitating his left arm, the only one he has free.

"The stere," Jean-Paul ventures.

"Wmmm," roars Porcher. The arm flails the air with increased vehemence.

"Mama," Madeleine pleads, "I don't remember anymore what comes after 'this day.'"

"The decaliter," Jean-Paul now tries, and then, "the pentagon . . . "

"This child's a half-wit," Porcher exclaims, pulling a dripping nose out of the funnel, then hurriedly plunging it back in again.

"Our bread," Madame Porcher completes. "Our daily bread."

Give us our daily cooking and washing to do. Give us our eight hours a day in the office. Our four hundred and eighty minutes in the office and our ten minutes of inhalation. The clock, the coal scuttle, and the gas meter. Our daily dose. Give us our daily slaps, our prayers, and our arithmetic. The gram, the centigram, the milligram, the millimilligram. And lead us not into temptation. Loulou, come on now, lift your arms. Take it again from the top for me, my lad, and deliver us from evil that's not what it's called now listen here if you don't lift your arms you're going to get one across the face pray for us poor sinners Milou could you pass me a towel the decagram the hectogram no not that one a blue one this day the kilogram this day this day this day I warned you you'd get something to cry about . . .

"I can't remember what comes after 'our daily,'" Madeleine shouts.

"As at the hour of our death," Madame Porcher shouts back, brandishing a washcloth above frantic Loulou.

At the hour of our death . . . Which will come after all these hours of our life that we'll have spent scouring pots, copying bills, raising children for the sake of pots and bills . . . These hours of our life with which we haven't done much, and look how it's already grown threadbare, this life of ours, and worn, and frayed, like the jacket you see on a bureaucrat. We've been wet by so many rains. A lot of them fall on a man over the course of his life. Fall on the sort of lives we have, us little people in our little world, a world of little troubles and rickety hand-to-mouth existences. On Iseult's scared and bumbling life. On Porcher's life. On the life of the two Old Folks who ask themselves for what purpose they could ever have been put here in the first place.

The Old Guy was an accountant way back when. He's a colleague. He has beautiful handwriting. It earns him compliments: these days it's his sole source of pride.

"He isn't good for anything," the Old Lady says in her hushed and furious voice.

Evenings, on getting back, I sometimes spend a moment with them in the kitchen downstairs.

First you have to walk down a hallway where there is a cold rancid odor that I recognize: it's the odor of my childhood, one I never got rid of—an odor I have in my blood like an old dose of syphilis. After that, you step into a large, almost empty room: table, three chairs, an oven—the indispensable minimum. All of it of a meticulous, miserable neatness.

As soon as he sees me the Old Guy takes off his cap in fumbling haste. You can never be too polite when you're poor.

The Old Lady, while going on with her ironing (people give her little odds and ends to do, out of charity), runs down a list of her woes for me. There's the matter of the rent and the doctor, and of a brother of hers who's a road inspector. I'll have had a lifetime of hearing about doctors and the rent. The Old Guy listens humbly. He's not good for anything. The daughter is sitting by the stove, staring at us who possess the indifference of water.

"You can imagine, with my poor daughter . . . "

The daughter smiles, she smiles an intolerable smile, aimed at no one, and which doesn't look as if it belonged to her.

"She's not a bad girl," the Old Lady says. "It's just that nothing's to her taste. You've got to tell her to do everything: She sits there all day long just the way you see her, without budging. No point talking to her, she doesn't answer, or else only to say yes, no. Ah, there are days when you wonder what ever brought you to this place."

What brought you was to iron out clothes. Iron out your troubles. Iron out your days. Iron out all your footsteps, today's, tomorrow's. Run the iron over all your words, all your sorrows. Hour by hour, until the hour of our death.

We belong to the same race, these people and I. With a fraternal disgust I observe the Old Guy's doddering head, his cap and his slippers. I'll look like that after a certain time.

And then will come the hour of my death. A wreath of glass pearls offered by the personnel at Busson Brothers. The owner's speech. The owner makes it his duty to pronounce, over their graves, a speech eulogizing his employees. You can count on that. After having faithfully served the sparkling-water trade we are entitled to a funeral oration. You know the words in advance because the same ones are used each time, they never wear out. The owner merely changes the name and a couple of dates. There is nevertheless an important moral privilege herein. Not everyone can boast as much at the hour of his death.

My Uncle Ulysse, for instance . . .

My Uncle Ulysse had become a no-account thanks to bad luck and drink. But my father liked him anyway, and in our family we told the story of how he made the trip to Brest, which cost a lot, simply to be at his burial.

Those particular burials take place at dawn, when cities are still asleep. The poor are buried in a hurry, discreetly. My father spent part of the night sitting on a wooden bench in a railway station, so as to avoid the expenses of a hotel. At first light, he went to wait near the hospital. He saw a hearse come out and followed it.

For him it was a heartbreaking thing, to be there all by himself, in those streets where he knew no one, behind that wobbling black rattletrap. The coffin once unloaded at the cemetery, he went to a neighboring café to warm himself up before heading back to the station, and because he felt the need to speak to someone about his brother Ulysse who was no worse than the next man, but who had been out of luck when he hooked up with that woman, a real bitch, and that was where it all started from.

While chatting with the man running the café, my father found out that in the morning there were often several paupers' funeral processions. Oddly, that hadn't occurred to him. He ought to have done some inquiring. So he went back to the hospital to find out. And it was just as he had feared: the coffin he had followed wasn't the right one.

> *The inconsequential writer recounts his*
> *inconsequential life.*

> —**ALBERT THIBAUDET**

That's what I do, evenings, at my place. I say "my place," even though there's not much in it that belongs to me—my slippers, some books, a spirit lamp. The rest belongs to the Old Folks. The shaky chest of drawers, the chair, the enamelware basin: I get that with the rent, twelve hundred francs a month. I don't know who used these things before me, what sad faces the murky mirror reflected, what bodies sought their peace in this iron bed with brass knobs on the bedposts. It's better this way. I don't care about heirlooms and family furniture. A twelve hundred-francs-a-month room, that procures you a reassuring feeling of anonymity. You're always too visible, too distinct. Here I'm truly just anybody at all. The ordinary guy who moves quietly among objects, without making any sort of commotion.

I smoke. I sink into one long daydream about other people's lives. I shuffle and reshuffle memories like cards for a game of solitaire. And when I've had enough of these musings, I reach for a sheet of paper and start writing out words. Idiosyncrasy of a solitary man. To sit down in front of some paper and to write words on it. Some people cut out the pictures in magazines. Others look at travel agency brochures or at maps. To each his pleasures. With me it's words. I try, with words, to summon up moments, faces, fragments of existence. My tastes have always been in that direction. To set words next to words, seriously, carefully. Seeking the shortest path from a period to a semicolon.

Bourladou thinks I am writing a book. I'm not sure how he got that idea into his head. You'll end up publishing us something one of these days, he would say with a perspicacious wink or two.

In the beginning I neither admitted it nor denied it, I didn't handle it well. For it was a flattering supposition, basically. It tickled old vanities inside me. It gave me a touch of importance and mystery. And, little by little, by dint of talking about it, it became an open secret that hidden somewhere up in my room was a manuscript that was quietly growing like a pumpkin under the leaves.

An innocuous little falsehood, but which took on consistency. Gathering nerve, I enter into the game. Before long I am confiding in Bourladou as to how my work is advancing. Evasively, to be sure, guardedly, with reserves and modesties.

I say that I'm moving ahead, that I feel I have what it takes, that it's all taking shape; or, on the contrary, that I'm in a difficult period, that I've stopped producing anything worthwhile—and those kind Bourladous comfort me.

"It'll bring you in a pile," Bourladou assures me.

"It's a novel, right?" asks Madame Bourladou.

"A kind of novel. More like a chronicle . . . "

"Oh. A chronicle . . . "

"Or an essay, if you prefer."

"An essay? . . . What do you know . . ."

"Well, a book in which nothing happens. People are writing a lot of books like that at the moment, you know. No plot, no particular story: just experiences, encounters, just . . . "

"I see, oh yes," Madame Bourladou declares.

"Curious," Bourladou says, "that's not what I'd have thought."

They'd like to know the subject: but there isn't what you could call a subject either. And the title? Tell us the title at least, Bourladou pleads.

"Well, you know, the title—that's the last thing you come up with."

"Of course," Madame Bourladou nods.

Now and then I pay Madame Bourladou a visit. The whole

extent of my intercourse with high society. She welcomes me with a little girl's gurglings of delight. Upon her creamy countenance a rapturous expression. But we haven't seen you for an eternity. Whatever has become of you? Of course, of course you are going to stay for a cup of tea . . . Madame Bourladou appreciates my conversation. With me one can tackle the larger subjects. Literature. Art. Madame Bourladou knows the names of several modern painters. She reads *Le Figaro littéraire* and novels in which it is said of the heroine that behind her filmy corsage her bosom is quivering. She knows some poems by heart, which she recites in a velvety, shivery voice:

Je n'entends que mon coeur qui bat
Tout bas tout bas tout bas tout bas.

"Lines by Aragon, my dear. It can't be helped: for all his being a communist, he's still a great poet, you can't take that away from him. As I am always telling Athanase, it's all the same to me what your politics are, all I look at is talent. What is making you smile?"

Madame Bourladou allows me originality, independence, and extensive knowledge. A pity that in my nature there's a denseness and a vulgarity that do not escape her. That urinal, for example . . . I ought to know that a urinal is not an object to be alluded to in someone's living room.

I resort assiduously to the urinal on the rue des Deux Eglises. At six in the evening, leaving Busson Brothers, we never fail to step inside, my colleague Porcher and I. In there I find ample wherewithal for reflections on the human species and on the act of writing.

Judging from its scalloped and emphatic style, the rue des

Deux Eglises urinal must date from the last years of the nineteenth century. With the passage of time, it has become rusty, dented, dilapidated. A dismal stench emanates from it.

"It hurts one to look at that," growls my colleague Porcher.

He deplores the slackness—that's his word—of a municipality that neglects public buildings to this point. "At the town hall they call themselves socialists, and they're not even able to repaint their pissoirs." I grant him that a can of paint would be quite enough to give back a decent and even fetching appearance to this melancholy assemblage of sheet metal.

"A coat of gray, that's how I see it," I say.

"Green would be my choice," Porcher says, "it's cheerier."

For a moment we contemplate, he and I, the agreeable effect a regenerated urinal would produce against this setting of plane trees and bourgeois facades. After which, we enter. We have ourselves a little piss. While pissing, we hold forth on urban renewal, hygiene, and local politics.

To piss, to palaver that way, quietly, peacefully—turn up your nose at it if you like. But even so it's a pleasure that counts. To piss unhurriedly, one's day's work done. I may take my own good time. No one is going to disturb me. At my age you appreciate such satisfactions. Because you know that even to have this is to be in luck. You've been done a little favor, they've temporarily lifted the restrictions. It's precarious, it may not last.

I haven't always had it, the right to piss. I remember those roads in Pomerania where we were being driven forward by the Germans not so long ago: forbidden to stop, forbidden to piss. I remember the cattle cars . . . We could bang on the sides as much as we pleased, the sentries wouldn't open the doors. You had to relieve yourself in an old tin can we handed from one to the next.

Memories of that sort, I have lots of them. (Everybody does.) Having them is useful. They quietly arise and add reinforcement to an otherwise thin everyday life, give it weight and substance.

"It's like this filth here," declares Porcher, standing beside me. "Ought we to tolerate it?"

Thus does he designate the profusion of drawings and inscriptions that clandestine urinators have strewn upon the urinal slate. A monstrous erect phallus. A preposterous welter of avowals, insults, and denunciations.

Indeed, right before my eyes is the picture of a coupling, unskillfully but precisely rendered. The author has indicated his intentions by means of a caption in capital letters: FLOUCHE SCREWING WITH WIDOW LOUCHERE. One may add that numerous allusions to the public and private life of Flouche are to be found elsewhere in the rue des Deux Eglises urinal.

On the whole, nothing of the unexpected in these scribblings. They've been the same for centuries. Pictures and words, no significant change. They are repeated, from urinator to urinator, from urinal to urinal, down through the ages. Attesting to the same need for the secretive, for the illicit, and for profanation. The same furtive protest against prohibitions and taboos. We see there an invincible tradition, one of those primitive and fundamental phenomena that sociologists would ponder if sociologists pondered. The sociologists, the psychologists, the novelists, all those who profess to give us descriptions of our fellow man. And one of the places where you can get to some degree an exact idea of your fellow men is in this run-down urinal, as peaceful and echoless as a confessional.

I think about the people who slink into these beggarly refuges, a bit of chalk in their pocket, listening for footsteps, scared half to death. Not only little mischief-makers. Why not respectable people also, people of mature years, fathers of families, like my colleague Porcher?

"You don't find this instructive?"

"I don't see what you're getting at," Porcher replies, given over to dandling the very last drops of urine from his member.

Porcher, too, even he must sometimes be visited by the desire to clear the dregs from his soul. To be invisible, to be true, to be oneself; and at the same time to be present to others; to reach them, to establish oneself in the consciousness of others by means of confession and scandal. I picture Porcher, with his raincoat and his imitation calfskin briefcase, surrendering himself to the delights of anonymity. He hastily sketches some outsized testicles. If anybody were to see me, dear God, if anyone suspected. Or else he writes that Flouche is a low-down character, and that he'll get what's coming to him.

"Why are you laughing?" Porcher asks. "This stuff strikes you as funny?"

"But I'm not laughing," I say.

"What you were doing is laughing, I'm telling you," Porcher says.

Now we are outside again. We hang about a while, chatting next to the woeful urinal. The damp plane trees along the boulevard Désiré-Lemesle gleam softly. To our right we see a few 1940s ruins. They've acquired an agreeable look because of the grass and wildflowers sprouting among the stones. In former times the Select Cinema stood there. A little farther off is the place du Président-Doumerche, with its memorial to the dead.

"We French are far behind the times," Porcher says.

He describes for me the urinals he's had occasion to observe in the course of his travels. In Brussels, in London: marvelous underground urinals, in white tile. Clean and unadorned, scientific. Urinals of that sort nip bad thoughts in the bud. They can serve no purpose other than the precise ones that justify their existence. No suspect dream could possibly attach itself to their uniform, hard, dazzling, candid surfaces.

Porcher coughs painfully. "Damned rhinopharyngitis, maybe I'm smoking too much." We say so long. He walks off at a brisk pace. With him he carries away his dream of modern *pissotières* in an aseptic universe. He heads for the brick house and the patch of garden where he cultivates his lettuce, his children, and his rancors. It's on the outskirts of the city, where the rents are lower. I watch him disappear. His back expresses intransigence and civic virtue.

*The French nearly always choose the right
spot for their urinals.*

—HENRY MILLER

So I spoke of this urinal to Madame Bourladou.

On that occasion she had some sort of old man sitting there in the depths of a big armchair. You could have taken him for a retired major: he was bristly and decorated. But he wasn't a major: he was a president.

"Solange, you will bring the President a glass of port."

A sly, disheveled little tart bustled in with trays. Madame Bourladou kept a close eye on her.

"That girl breaks everything she touches. If I were to tell you that it reaches the point where I sometimes wash my teacups myself . . . "

The president emitted a plaintive groan at the thought of Madame Bourladou's fingers with their enameled nails having to perform those trivial chores. Deplorable times.

"Cups handed down to me by Maman," Madame Bourladou was saying. "Genuine Dresden. I am very attached to them."

Minding what I was about, I sipped a little tea from the genuine Dresden. I ate some petits fours lacquered pink and green. And now the conversation was already rising to higher levels. Madame Bourladou wished to know whether I had heard the lecture by Monsieur André Loufiot, who, for the elite among our fellow townsmen, had come to discuss love in the writings of Stendhal.

At first I sought refuge in an expression of evasive distaste: bah. No, I won't be disturbed for such stuff. Pressed to explain my position, I pointed out the unseemliness of allowing that academician to monkey around with Stendhal in public. Madame

Bourladou voiced some "ohs" and "reallys" in protest. That's when I spoke of the urinal.

I said that I esteemed this Monsieur Loufiot a lot less than I did the fellows who decorate our city's urinoirs with chalked inscriptions. They at least yield to an authentic need to express themselves. And their naive messages testify to a wonderful confidence in the magical power of words. For example, in order to write in that way that Flouche is a low-down character and that he'll get what's coming to him, you must attribute a mysterious virtue to language. You must believe that through signs one attacks Flouche's being itself. In this rudimentary and impassioned literature one is able to measure all the primitive violence that is implicit in the act of writing. And a writer who doesn't feel in himself a little of the wizard and caster of spells doesn't interest me at all.

Ridiculous remarks, although they rather satisfied me when I brought them out. Ridiculous and misplaced, in poor taste. From the old man's armchair had risen a groan, a brief one, but one that spoke volumes. Madame Bourladou composed her indulgent smile, a somewhat pained, a faintly pinched smile.

"Now you, of course, we all know what interests you. Books . . . Books like those by that American, a pretty specimen, who has been taken to court by the way, which will teach him . . . "

Miller, of course. Madame Bourladou will never forgive me for Henry Miller. Yet it was she who wanted to borrow my *Tropic of Cancer.*

"You will be very shocked, I'll swear to that."

"Come, come, my dear, you take me for a schoolgirl."

She hid the book in her wardrobe, among chaste edifices of knickers and slips. "Because of the children, you understand. Jacques pokes his nose everywhere, imagine him running into this." (Jacques is twelve years old; he reads *Tarzan* and *Jim the Strangler,* suitable reading for his age.)

"I may be on the old-fashioned side," Madame Bourladou

told me, "but frankly, I don't understand the pleasure you are able to derive from reading such . . . things that are . . . "

I prompted her: "Obscene."

"Precisely," Madame Bourladou said, "such obscene things. What are you laughing about?"

"Nothing," I said. "An idea."

A groan came from the armchair. It was peremptory, determined, meditated. Out of it you could have shaped maxims, possibly alexandrines: "Where decency is not, beauty there is none," or some other such straitlaced formula.

"I'm sure that to you it's going to sound stupid, but the role of a writer, if you want my opinion, is to teach confidence, hope . . . to put forward an image of man that is . . . "

I suggested: "Exalting."

"Yes," Madame Bourladou said, "an exalting image. Whereas everything being published today is so vulgar, so ugly. It's not even written in French, nothing but slang, coarseness. Also it's all hopeless . . . They soil everything."

The groan from the armchair had overtones of excessive depression, and Madame Bourladou offered me some petits fours.

"Well, I do believe Athanase is here," she announced.

And Bourladou did indeed walk in, and a cordial tumult immediately filled the room. Why, you're here too, are you? President, things moving along all right? Solange, my little girl. We'd thought you'd died, you know, it's been such a while. Solange, for God's sake, are you deaf?

"Darleeng," Madame Bourladou murmurs.

"What have you been talking about?" Bourladou asks. "About literature, I suppose?"

"Your friend has such unusual ideas," says Madame Bourladou.

"Him?" Bourladou rejoins.

While gobbling petits fours, he asked me how I was doing

with my book. I answered that I felt all right about it. That I had just ended a chapter which had been giving me trouble.

Since we have been talking about it, my book must have grown to a good six hundred pages. And there are moments when I am almost able to believe in its reality. After all, the things I jot down, in the evening . . .

But no. You don't write books that way—haphazardly, without order or continuity. Books aren't put together out of that. All I know how to do is look at my life, and it's an uncharming spectacle. My life, or the brainless, busy, and fearful lives that adjoin my life. I don't find significance in them, no recesses or undersides. Which plainly shows that I'm no novelist.

If I were a novelist, beyond scattered actions, beyond the nullity of words and gestures and of all these sticky appearances, I would knit everything together with some coherent, comprehensive image, dense, fraught with meaning and tragic content. In it one would be able to discover a vision of the world (serious critics use the German term to sound still more serious). It's the hallmark novelists are recognized by—they put our scattered, futureless existences into contact and conflict, they furnish them with a direction, an added dimension, with all kinds of repercussions and resonances.

Even a Madame Bourladou . . . The incarnation of emptiness. Forty years of good manners and enameled smiles. Forty years of tatting, marital fidelity, and collecting recipes. Distinctive mark: the passion for products for maintaining the home. In the broad sense of the term—everything helpful to the maintenance of copper cookware, conversation, human skin, bourgeois intelligence, and Louis XIV furniture. And yet.

Yet it would be enough for a writer, a novelist, a true one, one of those whom the newspapers praise for his profound understanding of the human soul, in short, somebody in possession of a truly pathetic *Weltanschauung*. Were the attentions of one such person to be trained upon her, that would be enough for Madame Bourladou to turn into a monstrous node of complexes and repressions, the mysterious point of insertion for grace or perdition, the source of a family tragedy, and the site of a dreadful metaphysical debate.

But I, all I succeed in seeing is a lady moving past her prime, who is taking on weight, who has just bought an American gadget to combat a double chin.

Too bad. French literature, thank God, can do without my services. French literature, one is pleased to be able to say, has no manpower problems. It is not short of hands. We have them for every taste, for every job. We have the anxious sort, the world weary, the tough and the tender, the snappy dressers, the department heads. We have officials in ceremonial garb, for centennials and inaugurations of busts. We have the anarchists who wear jonquil-yellow sweaters and who are drunk at eleven in the morning. Those who are well up on the imperfect subjunctive, those who use the word *shit*, those who have a message to deliver, and those who are the guardians of the national tradition. Mailmen, policemen. Those who make me think of my cousin Virgil, who was no good at anything, who was engaged in nothing: so he joined up, and by and by became a sergeant—that's what engaging yourself leads to. You have *littérateurs engagés*, engaged writers, encaged writers. There are those whom black becomes, those who prefer pink, or those who incline to the red, white, and blue. And the psychologists, the pederasts, and the humanists, the kindly spirits, and the children of the people who cannot resign themselves to possessing so much culture all for themselves; and the Nietzschean moralists who were brought up in an institution out in Neuilly. We have writers of every description, it goes on and on. We have those who insult the dead and who besmirch the French army, and who then fall in step, and for whom an order is not a joking matter. We have our Stakhanovites who build you your thirty-volume novels, and inside them there's the entire age, with tables and methodical indexes to find your way around. Those who tour the provinces giving lectures, with three anecdotes and a moral couplet planted on top of each like a plaster bride on a wedding cake. And the little youngsters who talk all the time about their generation. And if they recount in two hundred and twenty pages how they sired a child on their mother's maid, that becomes the saga of a generation . . .

To begin with, it tickles me to hear them talk about the spirit of a generation. Look at those little lads squirming inside their pullovers. Just listen to them. No, we are not like our elders, no. We're a defenseless, whacked-out generation, etc. I have read that a hundred times. Or the opposite: we who are big on health, energy, simplicity, etc. Nowadays they cite Kafka, or Sartre. In my days it tended to be Freud, or Gide, or Rimbaud. Generations need proper names.

I, too, would have some proper names for citing. Those of Barche, Craquelou, Ravenel, or Pignochet. Men my age, men of my generation. They didn't write books, and they're not talked about in books. They were shovelers of earth or cement. We were mobilized together: a fine occasion to experience what in truth a generation is. War takes care of bringing generations together and separating them. Recruitment bureaus arrange men in layers as distinct as geological strata. So-and-so, contingent such-and-such. At least it's clear. Each where he belongs, in a layer of men born just about the same time as he. There's his generation for you. Present, weighty, concrete. For months on end I was able to observe it, that generation of mine, in those languid villages of the North.

What is certain is that everything that has been written about its uneasiness, its disarray, and its spiritual quests did not concern Barche or Pignochet, did not concern Ravenel or Craquelou. About such stuff they didn't give a damn. They, too, had had their youth, their misery. But no original misery. Apprenticed out at thirteen, kicks in the ass, the daily liter of red, the years on the job, the days in the hospital, the months on unemployment, that doesn't rate as very new.

The whole of my companions' past was made up of common difficulties. Dig as deep as you like, there was nothing to get at down there but the commonest of common difficulties. An experience as old as the hills, rock-hard, dateless. The same one their fathers and the fathers of their fathers had gone through before them. Each gets his turn, and it never changes. The same servitude, the same rotting within everyday shittiness.

Same joys as well, short-lived joys, furtive, humiliated, and mutilated joys.

Here I am yet again with the memory of the baby carriage. It stood at the roadside, shoved crookedly in amid the grass and mud. Not a soul around. Nothing but the vacant road, the plain become a slough, and that little spot of black. A cheap carriage, one that had plainly served for a good many kids. The rain was trickling down the oilcloth hood. Inside you could hear a baby's whimperings. You were reminded of the way in which popular novels used to open, stories about abandoned children. I drew closer to see what it was all about. Only then did I notice that there was yet something else down at the bottom of the ditch. At the bottom of the ditch were Craquelou and his wife; they were making love.

Craquelou, from Company Five. His wife had come to see him, with the little one. That was prohibited.

"I have strictest orders on this subject," Captain Lebiche repeated. "The very strictest orders."

Slowly, sorrowfully, he shook his head, that head of a sheep teeming with orders. This didn't prevent certain wives from figuring out some way to join their males for a few clandestine hours.

"If I ever catch one of them," the captain threatened. "Those sluts don't seem to be aware there's a war on."

Barche, the company philosopher, would comment: "In wartime, dear boy, you haven't even the right to make use of your balls like the regular run of mankind. But don't let it get you down, she'll find a guy to fuck her, you bet she will, that old lady of yours."

The spouses had to be kept out of sight, hidden, accomplices in the villages had to be bought. That meant expenses. Craquelou, who couldn't afford a quiet corner of a room, got off in a roadside ditch. It was annoying on account of the rain. Whatever, he hurried it up. Otherwise there wasn't anything about it he wasn't prepared for. Craquelou knew that this is the way things are, that you take your pleasure anywhere you can, when you can, on the run, when you are a guy like him.

And there are plenty of guys like him. You need but think about them for the problem of generations to take on its exact dimensions. That problem, and a few others, too, that literature has been dwelling upon.

"The execution will take place tomorrow.
Defendant, do you have anything to add?"
"Sorry," he said, "but I haven't followed
the case." And he went back to sleep.

—HENRI MICHAUX

I really shouldn't have let Bourladou believe that. This temptation to appear smart. But also he was irritating me, that Bourladou. One of those people who knows everything. Full of contempt for me because I am incapable of holding a conversation about wheat futures and soccer championships. "There isn't any fun in chatting with you." He sails in, plunks himself down. He reeks of importance and aperitif.

"Have a look at these shoes. What do you think?"

I look. I think that they have the rich color of newly baked bread, the color of well-waxed parquet floors in bourgeois interiors. I think that they decisively underscore the comfortable, rectangular silhouette of my friend Bourladou. I think about three black men in yellow shoes whom I saw one time in a rue de l'Odéon bistro.

"Well, you know," Bourladou says, "I paid three thousand eight hundred for them."

"Impossible! That much?"

I've blown it. Not enough stupor and indignation in my voice. My eyebrow wasn't raised high enough, my stare wasn't sufficiently wide-eyed. Difficult to obtain the right intonation, the proper facial expression. Bourladou shrugs. He launches into some tough-minded reflections on wholesale prices and retail prices. What he calls economic problems. "You following me?" I nod. Once again I see those three black men in the little café, with their friendly coal-black faces. "You are going to get the picture," Bourladou says. Nods. (Those delicate grays of the suits the black men were wearing: pewter gray, silver gray, lead gray.) "Middlemen are to blame for all that," Bourladou says. I acquiesce. I try to follow what he is saying, to put the three grinning, preposterous black men out of my mind. But they hang right in there. No way of getting rid of those three guys. It's idiotic. What's the intrinsic interest of three black men, compared with wholesale and retail prices?

"Can you beat that?" says Bourladou. "You aren't even listening to me. You're incredible."

He is furious. I find that I simply cannot admit to the black men. And he is already off and running again.

"By the way, there's a rumor going around . . . "

No rumor going around ever gets past him. The tenuous murmurs swarming and quivering down passageways, murmurs that slip, slither out between the stones of every wall: a town is alive with rumors. A continual stir of faintly sounding rumors that scurry like rats, like lice. They emerge from everywhere in this rotten town. Our venerable city, rich in its glorious past, as Flouche says in his speeches. Our old town smelling of dealers in secondhand goods, of hotel rooms let by the hour, of police stations. Pullulating with all sorts of furtive nastiness. Rumors that leak from old buildings, old souls. Rumors that run about, that flow about. Divorces, bankruptcies, shady deals, quarrels, miscarriages, cases of the clap. Bourladou collects all that. Very proud of being so well informed. Up on all the rumors going around.

"The wife of the Departmental Inspector of Schools . . . You know the wife of the Departmental Inspector of Schools? . . . "

"Madame Tapidour?"

"No, no, no. Tapidour is the middle-school headmaster. Now think: the wife of the Departmental Inspector of Schools."

"Oh, sure," I say, "a tall skinny person with yellow hair."

"That's right," Bourladou says, "and a pointed nose. Well, it seems she's dumped her husband. Yes, old man! And you'll never guess who she's run off with."

"With Tapidour?"

"Don't be silly. With Lazuli, old man. You imagine? The wife of the Departmental Inspector of Schools. With Lazuli."

I ask: "Lazuli, the auto mechanic?"

"Auto mechanic? What auto mechanic?" Bourladou wants to know. "Where have you seen Lazuli fixing cars?" His arms out-flung, he calls the whole town as witness to my stupidity—our old town—its notables, its mechanics, its cheated-on husbands, and everyone given up to the practice, the detection, or the exegesis of adultery.

I venture: "Lazuli, he isn't a red-haired fellow who has a glass eye?"

"Come on, snap out of it, that one died two years ago. I'm talking to you about Lazuli who has the furniture store on the rue Muguet."

"Right," I say, "you mean his brother."

"Not at all," Bourladou says. "They weren't even related . . . "

It's always that way. I become confused, get mixed up, am stumped. Like at my finals for the baccalauréat when a goateed old gentleman asked me the date of the Treaty of Utrecht. So then, sir, you do not even know the date of the Treaty of Utrecht?—his sardonic goatee leveled at me. I felt weak and guilty. Until the end of my life I shall have been the boy who forgets dates, the things one has to know, that everyone knows. "It's curious," Bourladou often remarks, "you're not interested in anything, you don't even read the newspapers." At such times upon Bourladou's face I am able to read everything that eyebrows, wrinkles, and chins can express in the way of discouragement and despairing irony.

Not even the newspapers. That which is printed in the newspapers, the news, essential bits of knowledge, what is being said and commented upon, the automobile accidents, the Radical Socialist Party's congresses, Flouche's speeches, what allows people to get together, to agree, to shout at each other, the ministerial crises, the movie actresses, the price of string beans and the Goncourt Prize and the record in the eight hundred, this information indispensable to human relations and human passions, trials, strikes, trade agreements, the solemn march of events, Truman, Stalin, I don't care about any of it. Not one bloody bit. And anyway, I get lost in all that, I don't understand it. And when I try to talk about it the way other people do, with other people, they can see right away that it's something I don't care about and just get more and more lost in. And Bourladou feels sorry for me. He being a serious man, normal, in close touch with the world around him, with life, with the times. The very image of competence, of pertinence. When that imbecile considers me, sitting in a chair, hands resting on his knees, sorrowing and superior, giving out that little snort of his, *hmph*, *hmph*, my thoughts are of the idea I must produce in others. It may be summed up in three words: a sad case. That does it, you can take him away now.

From there comes whatever pleasure Bourladou finds in my company. I am unable to conceal this from myself. He requires my mediocrity in order to be fully conscious of his own perfection. Of his intellectual quality. Of his prosperity.

Each time he leaves, it never fails, he plants himself in the middle of my room, he scrutinizes it as though he'd never seen it before. The dresser, the cracked basin, the shaving brush topped with dried soap. And then he makes that sad, stern sound with his nose.

"Boy, this certainly is a lousy place you've got yourself."

With my two hands I produce an evasive gesture of resignation. It's true that if you're talking lousy places, this place is lousy. A setting out of some proletarian novel. Especially the wallpaper, a reddish color, streaked with yellow fibrils, upon which the dampness has drawn a jumble of continents. "I don't understand," Bourladou says, "I really don't understand how you can live in this." Always hard to understand how people live where they do. In their room, in their skin, in their principles. At Bourladou's it's well-to-do, funereal, and waxed. Full of furniture. Mahogany, rosewood. Gleaming furniture, polished by the years, rubbed by Solange. A temple of steel wool, the vacuum cleaner, and chamois skin. Drapes, gilding, real marble and fake marble. The piano's a Pleyel, we paid two hundred thousand francs for it. Doilies on the furniture. Madame Bourladou makes them herself, she has exquisite taste. And piles of little doodads made of glass, porcelain, you're always afraid of breaking something. Vases. Flowers in the vases, Madame Bourladou adores flowers. That's what Bourladou lives in. In overripe comfort, flowery well-being. Bourladou lives in a sporty graygreen two-piece suit. He lives in his two hundred and ten pounds of human matter, meat and bone, guts and innards. He lives in his building contractor's round, fat, and moral life. And I'm a sad case, an ugly sucker. That's how Bourladou sees me and I know he sees me that way. Which establishes between us a bitter, hypocritical style of friendship, not without cowardice, and not particularly original when all is said and done.

These rights are of liberty, property,
security and resistance to oppression.

On top of everything else Bourladou is a hero. During the Occupation this selfsame man I see before me hid an English soldier for two whole days. The soldier, when he left, even gave him his cigarette lighter as a keepsake. Every time Bourladou lights a cigarette I get to hear the story of the soldier and the lighter. "What a risk I was taking," he says under his breath, as if staggered by his own grandeur. "We saw people being shot for less than that."

For my part, I couldn't be said to have risked anything at all. A boot or two in the ass, at the outside, or a rifle butt in the face.

"The Resistance," Bourladou tells me, "ah. You cannot imagine what we went through."

Meaning thereby that I spent that period tucked out of sight and taking it easy. Having a ball just twiddling my thumbs in my corner of Pomerania. It was the easy life all right: nothing else to do but leave it all up to them—to let go, to let yourself be pushed. We others didn't resist. When a guy would lie down in the snow because he had had enough of it and decided it wouldn't be worse to croak, a big raucous brute would come running up and start beating him. It was as simple as one, two, three: the guy got back up at once and got back in line. Without resisting.

The sentinels, too, with their rifles and their dogs, were guys who didn't resist. Seedy-looking old guys who were no longer good for anything except guarding men. They had their orders: bark, beat, drive the herd forward. In this world of destruction, that was all that was left: orders. Orders that came from else-

where, from a *Feldwebel*, and the *Feldwebel* got them from a lieutenant, and so it rose, following the chain of command, from
order to order, from lower rank to higher, from one threat, one
fear to a greater threat, a greater fear, it went on and on, you'd
lose yourself in the unthinkable, in an abstract, mechanical, and
infinite servitude . . .

The guards, the guarded—all the same. All caught in the same
inconceivable mechanism. We were the farthest down, that's
all. At the bottom. Underneath everything. Down where there
are no more problems—nothing finally but the insignificant
problems of slaves, like finding a little bit of water or stealing
potatoes, or patching together one's shoes with the help of a
piece of string. Yes, underneath everything . . .

That's what I drag along with me. Nothing but memories of
fear, humiliation, loss of self-possession. An experience that has
given rise to some rugged certitudes. You get to where you no
longer conceive of man as other than subservient, flattened,
crushed. And you stop even trying to understand. You cower in
your corner. The wisdom of the poor, banal and ancient as fear
and death. I am not a philosopher. One of those big thinkers.
Philosophers, they need only press gently on a word—on the
word *existence*, for example (I exist: what does that mean, "I
exist"?), and presto, the meditation starts emerging, laying itself
down like toothpaste. Even, creamy, unending. I was never
much at those games. My ideas about existence aren't complicated, and existing has seen to simplifying them still further.
Circumstances like the war, captivity—they eat away the words
and the fables with which you would like to mask the realities of
your condition. In the end, not much remains—this summary
bitterness, this passivity. If I were to confess this to Bourladou,
he would snort some of his reproving noises at me. He would
say: "I assure you there is more to it than that." He is perhaps
right, I don't know, I don't want to get into a discussion. He is

talking. He is sitting there, legs apart, shining and thick like a piece of summertime fruit.

"You're following me now, aren't you?"

Bourladou is telling his story. The cigarette lighter episode. The English soldier. What happened to him, Bourladou, and what happened to the others whom he agglomerates with his own adventure. The risks he ran, those he might have run. All that mixes into one stew for the feeding of his glorious vision of a universe dedicated to the practice of the very highest virtues. Bourladou arrays himself and swaggers in polite optimism. That's the way one must be. But I am unable to be that way. Something always slips in between, a screen that separates me from that world of pure enthusiasms and stunning acts.

"Are you listening to me?"

"Why of course I am listening to you."

"Well, you don't look as if you were."

True. I ought to be collected, meditative, stirred. But it so happens that I'm not vulnerable to chansons de geste. Nor to classical tragedies, to pictures of generals in uniform and military bands, to everything that uplifts you, swells your chest, makes you fall into step, inspires in you a wish to die while giving utterance to an historic phrase. A question of temperament, I imagine. Heroes stopped doing anything for me long ago. Why, when I was a kid there was already my grandfather and his war of 1870. Then came my Uncle Aurélien and his war of 1914. And now it's the same all over again. When you haven't had your own war, you're forced to listen to others tell you about theirs. Right. But I finally got my own war too. A pathetic and sordid war, that's the way it turned out. I don't tell Bourladou about it, I don't tell anybody about it, and I'd as soon forget the whole thing. The trouble is, though, that memories arise of their own accord. They sneak up on you, memories do, treacherous as leaking gas. The moment Bourladou turns his epic narrative on, the memories unfailingly arise. Memories in prose, not at all like Bourladou's. And prose, in a flash, blots out the epic.

In this way, the Yank comes to my mind. The Yank looked like a good-time street punk. An abundance of ideas was assuredly not one of his problems. A well-built guy, germ-free, question-free, his brain like a deep-freeze. I often think about that kid.

The rest of us stood around him, admiring him. Three dozen guys, in frayed greatcoats, greasy sweaters, and five years' accumulation of grime in the folds of our souls. "It's a wonderful sight, ain't it now," said the toothless man beside me. Absolutely: we'd eaten to our heart's content, nothing more likely to favor an indulgent conception of things.

To eat—for six months, that's all we had been thinking about. To fill our guts up with food, once and for all, to the bursting point. As soon as we had been liberated, we had gone prowling around the city, Ure, Chouvin, two or three others. With just that one idea in our heads.

The city had been what in former times was called a picturesque locale. Fifteenth-century buildings. Gothic arches, battlements, ivy. Now it was a city like all other cities. A few tons of bombs had modernized it: nothing left but pieces of wall and heaps of bricks.

"A fine job," Chouvin was saying.

Yes, a clean job. Intact houses, there was something wrong about them, suspect. Overfed. Full of stuff, like an intestine; all that stuff inside where humans hide their life. Whereas ruins, you at least can see through ruins, with one glance you take the whole thing in: a few lines, a layout, a sober indication. Ruins have sincerity, like skeletons.

Within this pulverized setting, we managed to unearth some margarine and potatoes. The wherewithal to put together a fabulous bucket of mashed potatoes. We fed on that for hours. Vignoche went off to vomit. So did I. Then Ure. And afterward we went back to eating. And then we slept awhile, and we ate again, threw up, and ate. And in due course we freed ourselves from the anguish of hunger.

Trucks and armored vehicles were moving on all the roads. A bare-chested soldier, sitting next to his jeep, gave me a pack of Camels. I strolled around. I smoked the tobacco of the conquerors. My freedom was as bumptious and snappy as a brand-new suit. That was when I saw the kid from the military police. He was standing in the middle of a crowd like the ones at country fairs that collect around the weightlifters or the hawkers of shoe polish. Opposite him stood four civilians, hands gripped behind their necks.

I asked what was going on.

"They're some Nazis who've been arrested," one guy explained to me.

The guy had a banged-up jaw and puffiness around the eyes. You could tell he was enjoying the scene. He told me: "Take a look at the hardware that Yank's carrying. Stuff like that is what we should have had in '40."

The hardware was a submachine gun, which the MP held clamped against his body with his elbow. There are men who find such objects exciting. The barrel of the gun swung gently up and down. It made you think of a cock. Of a guy toying mechanically with his cock.

One of the Germans, a big heavy man, was talking. He was talking fast. He was having to talk fast in order to explain things, to get out of a corner. And sometimes he loosened his hands with the purpose of making a gesture that might lend support to his words, add to their force. Instantly the machine gun's barrel would freeze with a living violence. A cock.

"They've changed their goddamned tune, the bastards," the fellow without teeth was saying.

For those four men it was all up. They were alone. There was that cruel steel organ. There was this wall of hostile men. And beyond, a destroyed city, a destroyed world. Four defeated men, with defeat all over their faces, moldy from fear. With their clothes, the pockets pulled inside out and hanging. Their dress of the defeated. Even the fabric spoke of defeat. It had become shabbier, drabber, uglier.

They had been frisked. At their feet, in the dust, pencil stubs, billfolds, a crumpled handkerchief, a few scattered cigarettes. Things they had possessed, made parts of their life—foreign to it now, dead. They took everything away from us. We have nothing left. We are nothing anymore.

"After the shit they put us through for five years," the toothless guy said, "it's their turn now."

Their turn to be afraid. Their turn for a bad time. The tide has turned, the fear, the misfortune that belonged to some now belongs to others, your luck changes, it's only fair. You always end up having your turn.

With his nonstop chatter the big German is a scream. The other ones are looking at him, their faces marked by straining attention and fright. The youngest may be about sixteen years old: a scrawny kid with ears sticking out from his head.

"You understand what he's saying to the Yank?" the toothless man asks me.

No, I don't. The MP doesn't either. They are words for nothing, that reach no one. Entirely lost. We are having a good time. The MP is enjoying himself. He, too, is shouting things. Insults or jests. And the barrel of the machine gun jiggles with an obscene liveliness.

"That Yank's a riot," the toothless man says.

A number straight out of a variety show. Something to file away to tell your buddies about later on, when you're back in Excideuil or Villefranche de Rouergue. "Them Yanks, that's the way they are," the toothless guy will say. Inside his calf's brain extends a dense mythology of gangsters, whiskey bottles, and hundred-story buildings.

The American is making the fun last. Machine gun in the crook of his arm, he sways to this side and then to that, doing a sort of dance—springy, nonchalant, facetious, ferocious—in front of the four fascinated men. Encouraging murmurs rise from the circle of overcoats and sweaters.

"Son of a bitch, he sure knows what to say to the Nazis."

"Scared shitless, those Nazis."

It may be that they aren't even Nazis. More likely some guys they'd have rounded up because of something wrong with their looks, or because a neighbor turned them in. Or for no reason.

That's what the heavy guy is trying to get across. That there's surely been a mistake. It can be looked into, there can be an inquiry. He doesn't have anything on his record. Neither do any of the other four. Just ask around. His voice grows ever more vehement, ever more hoarse. The American dances from one foot to the other while swinging his weapon. His voice is growing harsher too.

"It's going to get nasty," one spectator announces.

We move in closer, we can all feel it, the great moment is at hand. There's the MP suddenly flying off the handle. He starts yelling. The big Nazi is yelling. He's hanging in there, the big one. He's fighting to save his skin. The others are staring at him, faces wet, hands behind their necks. "Look out," the toothless man says. For the scene to be a complete success, there had to be this sudden tension, this explosion into hysterical, barmy dialogue. The Yank had sensed that. Something of an artist, that Yank. A guy who knew how to set up his effects and groom his denouements.

The denouement here was an unforeseeable and decisive movement: the MP shoved the barrel of his machine gun into the big German's mouth. Nobody expected that, that's for sure. One gesture and it was over with—a steely silence.

The machine gun had reared itself and with unerring brutality had thrust itself into the big man's mouth. Like a cock. We saw the big man's mouth dilate grotesquely and freeze that way. I shall see it for a long time to come—a tortured face where only the eyes, bulging from fright, were alive.

There was at first a moment of general stupor. Then from the toothless man came the word "Wow."

Whereupon the forty louse-ridden onlookers gave vent to a tempest of joy. It went on and on. The guy without the teeth, who felt I wasn't laughing loudly enough, kept encouraging me with slaps on the back.

It was, I now saw, a rather unpleasant scene. Victims are not pretty to behold. Nor, of course, are executions; and at these things the audiences are always ignoble. Thinking about it later on, I said to myself that what gives any such spectacle its value is its absolute explicitness. We were in one of those moments when life owns up, when you are able to see things clearly, when you see all the way to the bottom of them. Truth, that was what we were looking at. Truth unadorned and indecent. A truth that connected up with and implied other truths, terrible and absurd things that I had seen, and things I hadn't seen, which existed, which were yet a lot more absurd, a lot more terrible.

Afterward, the curtain may come down. You may well find yourself again before the walls and the words of a former time—you know the lying character of walls and words. You don't trust them; they are fishy. And you become like the guy they are after in detective novels, who steals about, on the watch for signs, a smoldering fear in his eyes. That's the way you live, like a hunted man, neglectful of the rules, ignoring the rules, and you do not even know what the rules are, nobody does. Should you ever be cornered, no point trying to fight or justify yourself. There isn't any reply, any recourse. A length of steel jammed between your teeth, that's how it ends. Or in some other way—

there are less rudimentary techniques: that Yank was just one of your self-taught fellows, a mere amateur.

I raise the shutter outside my window. I peer out at the streetlamp, the sidewalk, a poster: PUT YOUR CAPITAL TO WORK. A man and a woman are on their way home from the movies. They're saying that Madeleine Sologne was good, or something along those lines. The sound of footsteps fades. PUT YOUR CAPITAL TO WORK. Everything seems calm. You would swear nothing is going on. The night is lying. Some nasty trick is readying within the stillness. They've spotted me. Somewhere they've got a file on me, my description. Those bastards, wherever they are, are looking at the dossier. Though I may make myself unnoticeable, insignificant, hide in my room though I may, in the depths of the city and of the night, there is no preventing it. They'll have me sooner or later. The occurrence shall be an event without importance, irresistible, and faceless . . .

*They are nothing much, after all. They are
shoes that will become slippers.*

—VICTOR HUGO

At Bourget Airport we had sandwiches, Boy Scouts, nurses, red wine, and a picket of sailors standing at attention. There were more sandwiches, Boy Scouts, and red wine in a boulevard movie theater. And then I slipped off and went to look for a hotel on the rue de l'Echelle, where I had put up in the past. To be alone in a room—at that moment there was nothing in the world that I so much desired. I lost my way and had to ask directions from a guy who was walking by.

"Rue de l'Echelle's that way," the guy told me.

He had stopped in order to examine me. What he discovered was an unshaven individual, wrapped in muddy tatters and wearing a Polish forage cap a few sizes too small. The guy had correctly interpreted these shabby appearances: "So that's how you come back from Germany?"

I was coming back, like that. The guy wanted me to know that the Boches were never going to pay enough for all the harm they had done to us, and that in France we were too good. He kindly invited me to have a glass with him. I reproach myself for having refused him this pleasure. He seemed to be set on it. Just a quick drink, come on. I answered him that I was in a hurry.

"I can see that," the guy said, winking knowingly. "Hey, you've got plenty of time. Your old lady's been waiting for you for five years, she can hold out another fifteen minutes."

He was genuinely disappointed, a little offended.

"Oh well then, as you like. Anyway, the rue de l'Echelle's that way."

And that is how I emerged from the Second World War. Discreetly, modestly. At the time shopkeepers had a general's portrait on display. Poets were singing the "Marseillaise" and about the great days ahead, the rose, the reseda, and Elsa's hair—things that didn't concern me at all. I went back to my town. I resumed my rights. The right to Busson Brothers, to ration tickets, to the use of public urinals. The right to vote. Even the right to property.

I found that there had been changes in my town. A few bombs, in 1940, had introduced some odd zones of wreckage, weeds, and fences into the urban landscape. The moral geography above all had undergone disturbances. There had been shifts in moral standing. Persons of hitherto-unchallenged distinction saw themselves no longer respected by their fellow citizens. We had catalogued several dozen traitors and dirty bastards, among whom, I was surprised to learn, figured Dardillot, my eighth-grade schoolteacher. People were no longer saying good morning to Colamelle, of butter and cheese, who earned hundreds and thousands from selling high-fat nutrients to the soldiers of the Wehrmacht. No good mornings for Cantaloube, Dare, the Brandon-Targens either. I had to initiate myself into a new distribution of our spiritual riches. Anxious not to misplace my esteem, I questioned Bourladou: "Did they give the Brandon-Targens trouble?"

"Nothing very serious," Bourladou said.

The Brandon-Targens are a tribe of cloth merchants; pious behavior and dark attire. Well after it was deemed unsuitable, they had persisted in explicitly venerating the Vichy government. So, once the Germans were gotten rid of, they were made to understand things. All the Brandon-Targens, male and female, were marched through the streets amid a crowd animated by aroused and complex passions. Bourladou claims that I would have enjoyed the scene of those devout souls in mourning offering their sufferings to God and to the old Maréchal.

"It was worth going out there to watch, you know. Picture the Brandon-Targens who lives on the place aux Cailles being taken back there behind the barracks by some of the boys. They blindfolded him and shoved him up against a wall."

"And he was shot?"

"No, don't be silly. They were just kidding the whole time. A couple of kicks in the ass and they were even with him. But the old man was so scared that he still hasn't recovered from it, according to what I hear. Especially with his weak heart."

We have acquired some heroes and some martyrs too. Bourladou informs me, his objective tone that of a technician in heroism: "Chancerel was really splendid, you know."

Of Caucheron he says that he was someone you could count on for the rough work, but his attitude is one of reserve regarding the conduct of Fauchiez, who died in a concentration camp: your typical light-opera conspirator, according to Bourladou.

Louchère, too, did not return from Ravensbrück. And in addition there's Crise, Lamoue, Besançon, Marécasse, Mortimeur, Valache, others as well.

The whole town—leaving out the dirty bastards—feels linked to the victims by a mysterious solidarity. You have but to listen to people: everyone is discovering that he had his part, his deed, his hour of daring, his historic utterance. It is as a sign of this communion, and to assure the living in their irreproachable consciences, that a monument is going to be raised to the dead. Which will give us three of them.

We had the one for the 1870 dead; but the Germans unbolted its warrior with his chassepot rifle, all that being in bronze. There alone remains, on the place Rochefer, an enigmatic pedestal against which dogs come to piss.

We had the one for the 1918 dead. Fortunately it was carved entirely out of stone. Its soldier and naked child are just about intact. We can still get some use from it. That, for the time being, is where we lay the wreaths and deliver the Bastille Day and Armistice Day speeches. Nevertheless, the time has come to replace this old and outmoded testimonial to civic piety with a new structure, with new names upon it. The matter is being seen to. A committee of patriots was formed to this end, and a fund has been started; contributions are welcome from one and all.

Good old stubborn old human race: always ready to begin all over again, to give it another shot. To get up, shave itself, polish its shoes, pay its taxes, make its bed, do the dishes, wage the war. And all of it always needs further doing. It just keeps growing, it just keeps recurring on you: hunger, hair, dirt, war. And monuments grow on public squares, names grow on monuments. They always grow back, names do. You always find stone to cut names into, you always find names to cut in the stone . . .

Bourladou, naturally, is a member of the committee. He is on all the committees. He was born to be a member.

The committee has given itself a title: it is called the Erection Committee. At first, the word surprised Troude, who's not very sharp, and Doctor Fleuron had to explain patiently to him that it came from the Latin word *erectio*—I rear, I raise, I lift, I erect. Fine, all right, Troude said. Returning home he announced to his wife that he was a member of the Erection Committee:

"A member? . . . "

His wife sniggered unpleasantly.

"Certainly," Troude said. "Of the Erection Committee."

Madame Troude laughed out loud.

"I don't see anything funny about that," Troude said. "It's a word that comes from Latin."

From among divers projects for a monument that were put

before it, the committee selected the one in which the Resistance appears in the guise of a gymnastics instructor from whose wrists hang chains which, his pose tells you, he has just broken. The committee found the idea ingenious.

We are promising ourselves a pretty ceremony. Flouche will celebrate the dead, and once again shall our old town, rich in its glorious past, lie under the spell of his rhetorical periods. Those upon the official platform shall include Madame Louchère, widow of the martyr, presenting her pathetic veils to the wind and to the crowds her stony countenance, where her blued eyelids lower over a tearless grief.

"Is it a fact that she's Flouche's mistress?"

"You're asking me too much," Bourladou answers evasively. "Such has been the claim. Anyhow, it's a rumor going around…"

Flouche is a deputy in the Chamber, he has been a minister. His role in the Resistance has been of great help to him in his political career, although that role remains imprecise and has even prompted reactionary elements to formulate mean-spirited insinuations. You may contemplate Flouche in the newsreels, surrounded by dignitaries with stern chins. I would never have suspected so much ability in him, back in the days when he went around selling floor wax and polish for copper cookware.

No longer is he that fat, oily personage, not very clean, who used to take part in discussions between two games of belote. Upon emerging from obscurity he acquired density, his shoulders broadened. A certain negligence in his getup is still there— just what it takes to inspire the common man's trust (that maintains the militant's, the champion-of-the-people's style). But underneath you sense the compact, sober, and secretive figure of the statesman.

The look Flouche has given to his face, it's the crowning touch. Back in the floor-wax days I used to think he resembled a noncommissioned officer who was doing another hitch— puffy, lackluster. He has managed to turn the puss he used to have into an imperious mask, massive and harsh: it's Danton's face, the likeness is striking.

I ran into him the other day on the rue Sainte-Goutte. He truly looked as if he had stepped out of a history textbook. He was provided with an invulnerable glacis of historic majesty. His voice, the voice of Danton, filled the rue Sainte-Goutte with a din where calls to arms merged with the rumblings of a restive crowd. A youngster who had been kicking a tin can about suddenly stopped in order to observe our conversation.

Flouche asked me what I was up to.

"Still at Busson Brothers, I suppose?"

I was intimidated. I have never associated with statesmen. I only know, from having read the works of M. Jules Romains, that from them you may expect luminous and wide-ranging commentaries on the situation in the world today. When in the novels of M. Jules Romain a minister begins to explain things, you understand everything at once. You discover the consequences and the incidences, the underlying forces of the age, the hidden side of cards in the game, the behind-the-scenes picture, the false bottoms in the drawers.

But Flouche held himself to familiar considerations. He complained about his liver, which is doleful and swollen, and spoke longingly of taking the waters at Vichy. He told me something about a convention over which he had to preside somewhere in the Lot-et-Garonne.

"I'm dog-tired, my friend, utterly drained, a wreck . . . "

Danton's voice rolled oceanic waves of lassitude and melancholy. I understood him to say that he envied me my obscurity, my imperceptibility, my irresponsibility. He employed the expression "ivory tower."

"It's quite simple," he said to me, "a man like me, don't you know, does not belong to himself."

His wide-flung arms called upon all of the rue Sainte-Goutte to bear witness to this enslavement. Then passing by, Canon Coudérouille—brisk, gray, and angular—whisked off his cap. A man like Flouche belongs to History and to the Masses. Impossible to shirk the expectations of History and the affections of the Masses.

I was reminded all of a sudden of a public meeting Porcher had dragged me to long ago, when Flouche was appreciated by only a few dozen citizens lacking in social importance. A modest meeting, held in a small room hung with pink paper garlands, furnished with three flags and a record player. Those present called each other fascists and dupes. Flouche, gesticulating upon his platform, looked like a schoolteacher being ragged by his pupils.

He was shouting at the top of his lungs, but what he was shouting sank within the tumult. A few isolated words remained afloat—laboring classes, masses of the people. A woman with a big backside kept repeating: "Let him explain himself, come on, stop it, let him explain himself."

She turned toward me, and along with her I said that we should let Flouche explain himself. Flouche shouted: the masses will not permit. The lady wished to know what the masses wouldn't permit. She definitely belonged to those masses.

I, too, belong to them. People like me, like Porcher, like Iseult, like the two Old Folks, we cannot pretend to any but that collective designation and to that undifferentiated mode of existence. Our frail particularities are soon lost within a shapeless immensity. We are a homogeneous and indistinct substance—we are the masses.

"Well, it's been a pleasure to see you again."

Flouche had just tipped hats with Corchetuile the butcher, with Rudognon the bookseller, with several anonymous greeters. He held out his hand to me. A hand made to clasp the masses' innumerable hands, to punctuate the innumerable high points of campaign speeches.

A hand that did not belong to him.

Why should I succeed since I don't even feel
like trying?

Having left him, I walked back along the rue Sainte-Goutte. That Flouche, I was saying to myself, is someone who has come a long way in the world. One of Bourladou's expressions, to come a long way. Bourladou has come a long way, too. Not I; I'm still at the same point, I'm not moving.

"What are you up to?" Flouche had asked me. An odd question. I allow life to accumulate patiently, take on consistency, take on weight within me. It is clear that my existence is not what they call a success. I am about to reach forty-two. At such an age you are definite about yourself. You have things together, solidly together. What am I up to? Becoming a man of forty-three, of forty-four . . .

The name Flouche was flowering on new posters: in a few days Flouche will be giving a talk on the economic organization of Europe. Those who used the rue Sainte-Goutte would glance, and the name Flouche would dance for a moment in the minds of these anonymous Europeans, amid various unelevated concerns and some grubby calculations.

I heard a biddy girded about with feathers and woolens confide to another biddy similarly fitted out: "Fifty francs for three rolls, you must admit that's rather a lot."

"Oh, I grant you," replied the other nag, "but newspapers are expensive too, and besides, well, what can I tell you . . ."

If I understood correctly, the mounting price of toilet paper was the subject of their discussion. Those old ladies have tiny brains. Not unless broken down into the smallest fragments can economic problems make their way inside.

After the point where the rue Sainte-Goutte runs into the rue Douillet, all you can do is let yourself be borne along by the six o'clock rush flowing down to the place du Théâtre, along with all the Crédit Lyonnais personnel, the Monoprix sales-girls, and the employees from the Prefecture.

In front of Tripier Confectioners, a little male in a fawn-colored windbreaker had just stopped his bike near a young girl. He remained seated on his bike, one foot on the sidewalk, and he was eating an apple while talking. I admired his self-assured air, his unself-consciousness—I was never like that.

"He's not the kind who goes for the ball," he said, speaking with authority.

The girl seemed fascinated by this remark. Not pretty: a large pimply face, unevenly powdered. Saturday, he'll take her to the movies. Their choice, this week, is between three shows: *Cavalcade of Love, The Other One's Wife*, and *The Man Who Conquered Destiny*.

There's one I should go to see: *The Man Who Conquered Destiny*.

Walking onto the square, I felt I'd like to buy some flowers from the poor soul who stands near the Trois Colonnes café and chants all day long: "Buy my pretty carnations, buy my pretty carnations . . . "

What indeed can be her thoughts touching destiny? She's very large, very shapeless, done up inside layers of rags and tatters, and crowned by a scarf of yellowish madras.

"Buy my pretty carnations . . . "

It occurred to me that flowers would have a peculiar look in my room. They would not be in their place. They would introduce a false note, an incongruous display of life.

My room is the way it ought to be. It has that gray sour odor belonging to those places where many little existences have worn down one after the other. The Old Lady has judiciously decorated the walls with photographs. I often look at them: very old photos, faded, funereal, in blue velvet frames.

There is a couple being married: the groom's adornments include a circumflex mustache and an undertaker's frock coat. There are boys making their first communion; they look like convicts. Girls making their first communion. There's an infantryman respectfully holding before him, like a martyr his head, a pomponed kepi. I call him the Unknown Soldier. When Bourladou studies this military man in white floss-silk gloves, he never fails to sing:

A soldier is like his pompon,
The older he gets the sillier he looks.

So far as one can judge from his faded effigy, in the Unknown Soldier's character there was a happy balance of playfulness and sense of duty. This decent lad worried himself over questions of mess kits and gun grease. He would say, though without true rancor and more in order to sound like the others, that the sergeant major was a drunkard and a son of a bitch like you just can't imagine. Maybe he was lucky enough to become a store-keeper, or an officer's orderly. The rest of his biography disappears within a vaster adventure.

Like this one, the room I had as a boy was full of photographs. It's a taste widespread among the toiling classes. Practically the same photos: children making their first communion, soldiers and bridegrooms, similarly beflowered with a ceremonial smile.

I would ask: "And the little girl there, who is she?"

"Your cousin Blanche," my mother would say, "you know that perfectly well: the one who died of chest trouble."

Yet God knows that they tried everything in order to save her, the poor child. Including taking her on a pilgrimage to Lourdes. It was of no use.

"And the man wearing the collar with the bent corners?"

That was Uncle Ulysse, who had married a bad woman, and

then he had begun to drink, and finally they found him drowned in one of the basins of the port of Brest.

In this way, upon each of these portraits lay a sort of mist of bad luck, of calamity, of discord, of shame. In the overcrowded, creaking room, these pale presences introduced a murmur of tragedy, a train of premonitions, of muffled allusions to that suspect and precarious world in which a person would have to live.

I imagined Uncle Ulysse stretched out upon the stones of a quay, dirty water dripping from him, and all bloated. People were bending down to see better. A police officer was writing things in a notebook. I knew, through the illustrated supplement of *Le Petit Parisien*, that this was the way things proceeded.

"Mama," I would ask, "didn't anybody try to give Uncle Ulysse artificial respiration?"

"Be still," my mother would say, "go to sleep."

She would tuck me in, give me a kiss. She abandoned me to the shadows, shaking all over, a mite entangled in his prayers and his stories, midway between fear and dream.

Perhaps it is because of the photographs. As early as then I lost confidence, I gave up. They had done their best, all of them, the boy cousins with their shaved heads, the girl cousins with their stiff pigtails, my uncles with bent-down collars, they had put their whole heart into living, all their good faith, their unremitting effort. And it never worked out, things always went wrong. Might as well face the facts right away . . .

Yet we didn't lack ambition in our family. They were counting on me. My parents felt sure that I at least would get somewhere in life. I'm not too certain what they meant by that. At any rate, they assured me that getting somewhere required work and thrift.

"Plus schooling," my father added seriously, "schooling."

They hadn't had schooling. When I studied my lessons, between the stove and the sewing machine, they marveled at all that learning I was accumulating. With that, I would go far, they set their minds at rest. I went all the way to Busson Brothers, Sparkling Mineral Water.

Not enough work, probably. Or not enough thriftiness. Something in there wasn't going right, that's for certain. Or else there might have been something wanting on the moral principles side. And in moral principles my mother and father were well versed. They had learned them in the local primary school, around the year 1880. They had learned them along with the past participles conjugated with *être* and *avoir*; along with the names of the departments, of their prefectures and subprefectures, in alphabetical order.

A penny saved is a penny earned. Out of little acorns. A bird in the hand is better. A rolling stone. There's no getting away from it, you've got to believe in the whole package. Education exists as a block. If all that were not true—the proverbs, the principles—there would be no reason to believe in past participles and subprefectures. One wouldn't be able to believe in anything.

I have to admit that I was well brought up. Good principles at every meal. Throughout my early years there was no sparing either of advice or of cod-liver oil. Everything required to make me into a sturdy lad, armed for life. And despite so much well-intended precaution, I see myself at forty-two looking at the ledgers and invoices at Busson Brothers, beside my colleague Porcher. Porcher has four kids and grumbles about a government that isn't interested enough in large families. But I'm more the resigned type. I keep my trap shut.

So I am forty-two years old. Height: five feet seven and a half. They've got it in my army records. And thirty-seven inches around the chest. In an advanced society, everything's on record. If you wish information, if you are interested in finding out about yourself, you simply apply to the proper authorities. You consult the registers. No way of getting worked up about anything. You live within defined limits. As regards my intellectual capacities, I have a baccalauréat, section B, but I didn't pass the licentiate exams. That's recorded also. At least, this way, you know exactly what you're dealing with, you are provided with precise points of reference. I'm a clerk, I make my living by writing things down. At Busson Brothers, Sparkling Mineral Water. That's what situates me: I've got a modest situation. I cannot exaggerate to myself the position I hold in the world: a fifteen thousand-franc-a-month position at Busson Brothers. I know to within a franc what my value is. I am worth five hundred francs a day.

"You shall not hear me complaining," Bourladou is wont to remark.

Bourladou's are humble origins and he does not hide it from himself; rather, it is something he is even given to flaunting: son of a Flanders coal miner, scads of brothers and sisters.

"Oh no, I wasn't sent off to some secondary school, not I, and it didn't prevent me from making my way in the world."

He has the right to say so. Nobody will claim the contrary. It can be verified. Things looked at objectively, Bourladou has made his way in the world. Upon reaching the hour given over to digestion, favorable to the taking of stock, he gazes at the armchairs and the Pleyel, and Madame Bourladou in her lavender-blue housecoat. The candor of the lace doilies. The intimate gleam of the rosewood.

"Starting out from where I started out from . . . "

He lets himself slide to the very bottom of his childhood. Down there it's dark, it's wet. A cellar.

A mechanical marking of time in that mushy substance of childhood. The color of affliction and rain. Color of fear and soot. The smell of cellars. Dankness. You smack up against one wall, then against another. There's no way out. Walls everywhere. The invincible indifference of walls. It's in there that it all began. You wouldn't believe one could get out. Notwithstanding that, I did. I shake myself, I open my eyes, up I go. Everything resumes its place, everything arranges itself around me once more. Nothing's missing, it's all there. The armchairs, the Pleyel, the doilies, and this distinguished spouse who calls me "dahleeng":

"What are you thinking about, dahleeng?"

Bourladou is thinking that he has come a long way indeed. He contemplates that road which leads up to Bourladou. Again he sees the miners' brick tenements and the cinder sidewalks. There's a kid roaming around the slag heaps. A woman yells for him to come back to the house, his father has had an accident. In the kitchen his mother sobs in the middle of a circle of neighborhood women. Consider it a miracle that he got out at all, the women are saying. He could just as easily not have made it. Might have been better if he hadn't, his mother says. Considering where we're at now. Good heavens, you mustn't say such things. And the other fellow, you know, the other one's gone out of his mind. That's worse than anything, don't you understand. And that's just the way it always is in this goddamned work they do.

His father was caught underneath a cave-in, along with a mate of his. Thigh crushed to bits. It had taken ten hours of work to dig them free. "Rotten piece of luck," the father says when they go to see him in the hospital. His enormous, smashed-up head stirs upon the pillow. "Rotten piece of luck," he repeats once or twice, then withdraws into his rocklike silence. He's a man who doesn't talk. Only good for mining coal, getting drunk on Saturday night, and making kids. A taciturn giant, with sudden upsurges of violence. Once, when he was getting a bawling out from an engineer, he threw the man out the window. His father had listened quietly at first, his face blank, kneading his cap in his heavy hands. And then his anger arose, and things happened fast: they picked up the engineer nine feet below, in the courtyard, surrounded by broken glass. There again, a rotten piece of luck. He had had to look for work in other places. Nowhere were they eager to hire this colossus who demolished engineers: such behavior, to the extent it was tolerated at all, would make the exercise of authority difficult. For months on end he had been turned away, at pit after pit, at town after town, from one end to the other of this cruel country of brick and mud. His wife blamed him bitterly for their wretched plight. He could have given a thought to the fact he had children before acting like a fool. The father didn't argue. He didn't know how to argue. He was a brute, Bourladou's father, a sort of Neanderthal.

"I have been thinking about my father," Bourladou says in an earnest voice.

He has been comparing his own existence with that of the rudimentary creature his father was. He is measuring that distance between his father and himself—that long way in the world. And the meditative *hmph*s he expels from the depths of his armchair signify that a gentleman with guts always manages to take care of himself.

It's pretty clear that I have nothing in the way of guts, or not much. I have lacked the strong virtues that conduct a child of the people all the way to a snappy suit, to decorations, to polished furniture and a lustrous well-being. But that's all right with me, I've never expected too much. I'm simply noting the facts, that's all. I'm noting that I haven't made my way in the world.

And thuswise does mankind advance: with a few who are rich, with a few who are beggars—and with all its poor.

However, if I haven't made my way in the world, it's not because I haven't done any walking. I have done nothing but walk. Walked from my house to school. From my office to my room. That finally adds up to a fair number of steps. And there was military service: marching with the regiment every morning between the barracks and the drill ground. In step: one, two, one, two. I never succeeded in really keeping in step. It looks very simple—left, right. But I always fell a little behind, or got a little ahead. And it never eluded the drill sergeant's hearing, sensitive to everything that compromised the stern music of marching steps. In step, for God's sake. Left, hut, right, hut. We would march through an outlying district of unending garages and cafés. Left, hut. The maids, at the windows, would be shaking out their feather dusters. One, two, one, two. All it takes is one guy who has no turn for this to disturb the powerful affirmation of two hundred and fifty soles coming down as one upon the pavement of a street on the edge of town.

"Where the hell did they find a jerk like that one to stick me with?" the sergeant roared.

He roared those words out of conviction, out of professional conscience, and also to impress the maids. Sometimes he referred to me as "an intellectual with brains about the size of my balls," in order to teach me modesty. Wherein he showed himself intelligent: one cannot learn modesty too early or too well. The sergeant's scorn put things into focus. It is useful to get the

The Cattle Car

56

idea into your head as quickly as possible that you count for nothing whatever, that you have no importance at all. That prepares you for what awaits most men in existence. Subsequently you are less surprised. You're adapted, readied, all set. The sergeant's sober assessments constituted no more than an anodyne beginning, an innocent preamble to harsher experiences.

One day, it was some fifteen years after the sergeant, I stopped to take a leak against a tree. It wasn't allowed. You were to keep walking with the others, across absurd snowy plains, upon roads that led nowhere. Yelling guards were driving us on through that blasted snow, from one horizon to the next. No longer any question of marching in step. Ours was a wavering, disjointed progression of weary gray crabs. They cautiously lift and then advance now one leg, now thrust the other one forward, and begin again, patiently. That's how I was walking. Step by step. And with each step a monotonous suffering shoots deep into my body. My stomach hurts, my shoulders hurt, my thighs hurt, I hurt everywhere. And on top of it, this need to piss. I fought it for as long as I could. And then there was that tree by the side of the road, all alone in the empty landscape. A humble, decent-looking tree. I started in upon a voluptuous piss against that tree. Behind me the sluggish procession of crabs was continuing. And in an instant a sentry had come up, shouting at me. It took but one kick in the ass to boot me back among the crabs. The sentry was splitting a gut laughing. So were his buddies. It was pretty funny, all right, this limping guy who was trying to run while adjusting his soaked underpants. A guy who can talk about Picasso or Negro art, recite poems by Claudel. An intellectual with brains about the size of his balls. Right. Very funny. I began to walk along again. Step after step. Leg after leg. Left leg. Right leg. I'm used to it; I'm known for it, the obscure determination of crabs. This time it was at the far end of Europe. But there or somewhere else, it makes hardly any difference. It's all one and the same, as my mother used to say. You walk, you walk, and when all is said and done you're just where you started. I'm talking about people of my ilk, those without any guts. This is the case of a great many, we are surely the majority. We create an odd sort of immobile stir, with all our legs forever fiddling in emptiness.

When I have some time, in summer, I go to the public garden. It lends itself well to meditation upon all this. The behavior of crabs, I wish to say. They have a keeper there and observing him is instructive. An old-timer, a cripple from the other war. "I was wounded in the thigh and in Les Esparges," he says, making a joke of it. A godsend, that wound of his. Owing to that hole in his thigh he was given a pension, enough to get drunk on once a month. Then he got his keeper's job. A nice little job: not a damned thing to do except walk around the plots of grass. He's got his keeper's cap, his keeper's cane. He walks around the pool where twelve faded fish float in a circle. He walks by the botanist in stone (1794–1881). He walks by the automatic seesaw. He starts over: basin, statue, seesaw. Like that for a quarter of a century. Step after step for twenty-five years, and he's still in the same place. A satisfying symbol of my existence and of a good many other existences. Stick with it, old friend, stick right with it. Seesaw, basin, statue. You'll be at it forever. This is your place in the world. Your keeper's place. My place is over at Busson Brothers. Each one in his place. This world of ours is put together awfully well, when you give it some hard thought. The botanist is in his botanist's place, set above a little shrubbery and rock. The seesaw in its seesaw's place. The goldfish in their fishes' place, in their dirty water. Order extends over everything. The keeper keeps an eye on what has been put into his keeping. He keeps an eye on the grass, on the dirty water, on the broken mechanism. He keeps an eye on the guy in stone: no danger of anyone making off with their botanist.

Sometimes we chat a bit, the keeper and I. We understand each other. He told me that his daughter had been knocked up by a clerk in the town hall who won't listen to anything about marrying her. "It's one hell of a mess, I don't know what to do," the keeper tells me. He pushes back his cap to show the extent of the quandary he is in. I tell him yes, it's a mess all right, but what can you do, that's life. A practical formula. Short and practical. We employ it often, we do. It dispenses you from having to look any farther. It cushions the blows. It also proves that you think about things, that you know how things work. It's life, says the keeper. He squares his keeper's cap. Life, life. He lurches off with his creaking gait, his back askew. Life, life.

Some old people look his way, some old people solidly installed on the benches, comfortably enveloped in their old people's odor. You have the right to sit on the benches. There's no throwing stones into the pool; no picking flowers. But you can sit on a bench, remain there an hour if you want, two hours, whiling the time away, spitting now and then. To the park come some who are ailing, some in bad shape, people missing part of an arm or a lung. People on crutches, people in dressings, people with gauze and adhesive-tape bandages. The wife or the daughter told them to take a walk, it being cramped at home. They are in the way, wandering back and forth for hours between the bed and the stove. And, too, it finally gets to be disgusting, their smell of urine and medication. And, anyway, they'd just as soon be outside. Inside it bothers them to be a bother all the time. It bothers them even when nobody reproaches them for anything. The woman takes a dustcloth to the sideboard as if between the two of them, her and her sideboard, there were a score to be settled. You know what all that means. She shakes her rag out the window, she jabs the poker about in the stove. Then the man says he's going out for a walk. "Bundle up well," the woman nonetheless recommends, picking up an armful of dirty laundry. The man heads out to cough and limp with the neighborhood's other coughers and limpers. With one another they have conversations of their own sort. They talk about blood pressure, injections, suppositories, Social Security. There's one who explains that it is above all toward the end of the night that it begins to stifle him, but really, to the point where you'd think it was about to kill him, and he tries counting so as to think about something else, up to a thousand, sometimes, and even beyond. And another says that for him it's especially the coffee that's hard. The rum, the wine, all right, he doesn't mind. But let the doctor rant and rave, no, he is not going to be deprived of coffee. Concluding their sentences, their voices rise falteringly and then sink, the way a crab's legs do.

The keeper eavesdrops as he walks past. He thinks that that's life. He passes and passes again, thinks and thinks some more. Life. Life. "And now they've started talking about operating on me," moans a guy whose face is a grayish green. "Operating on me," the guy goes on; "I'd rather croak right away." With the tip of his shoe he digs feebly into the pathway's rust-colored sand. The keeper is thinking about a medical book, which he has at home, which he leafs through in the evening. It's nice, the way they have them in the book, livers, spleens, intestines, it's cheerful, dolled up that way in geranium and hydrangea colors. But inside a belly it must be pretty god-awful. In his mind's eye the keeper has a vague image of that sticky, crawling bundle of things one has inside one's belly. And then he tries to imagine the things that are now in his daughter's belly, those things that have started to live, to become stubbornly bigger, longer, and what will all that end up as? A little son of a bitch like that son of a bitch clerk at the town hall. A guy with straw-colored hair and a sly smile, who'll also do his dance and get girls pregnant, it won't ever stop, six of one, half a dozen of the other. Life . . .

The keeper works round the grass, step by step. He looks at a lady in a leopard-skin coat. The leopard-skin lady looks at her dog urinating at the foot of the botanist. The botanist is not looking at anything.

The botanist is above all that, above us. About nine feet above us. Established in the twofold immunity of stone and death.

To him we owe, so it is recorded on the pedestal, several papers presented to the Naturalists' Society of the Ardennes and a complete flora of the canton of Saint-Jacques l'Entourloupé.

To our studious compatriot the sculptor attributed lips in the shape of a trapezoid and the forelock of Monsieur Thiers. Solidly anchored upon his pedestal, protected by a municipal decree dated March 2, 1907, the botanist reminds the living, as they drag about, left foot, right foot, upon varix- and rheumatism-ridden legs, of the existence of ideal values. Culture, Knowledge, Erudition, the noble works of the mind. With the world around him he had only choice relations, exemplary in their graciousness. His thoughts, when it fell out that he had thoughts, danced, with a white butterfly's liveliness, amid Latin syllables, *lycopodium, tucilago farfara*. His had nothing of those sordid thoughts which the people down below, the people on the park benches, forever hash over. There are thoughts and then there are thoughts. The botanist did not ask himself, like my landlady, what we were put on this earth to do; he knew. The botanist's daughter was not seduced by a town hall clerk. The botanist's belly contained nothing but noble viscera. His was a distinguished belly, discreet, cozy, witty, and good company.

Not a belly like the belly of people who have no guts: that is, whose bellies have nothing in them but lots of crap which swells and rots, and which they talk about all the time. The botanist had the belly of a man of science and of a man of the world. There are bellies and there are bellies.

There are the bellies of men of action. Bourladou's—you need only look at it: now that's the belly of somebody with something to him. A large, substantial, guts-filled gut; a belly nevertheless without laxness, without arrogance. One that expresses dignity, plenitude, strength. Upon the downy material covering it appear wrinkles, as upon an anxious brow. Between waistcoat and trousers a note of intimacy and of good-naturedness is sounded when from time to time you catch a glimpse of poplin, soft of hue. But the overall effect is serious. Solid and serious. Bourladou's gut inspires in me the same spontaneous consideration, the same respect as the safety vaults and the facades of banks: there's something inside. In there lies the crux of it all. It takes a belly like that, with everything it encloses, those guts charged with conquering energy, in order that a boy starting out from where Bourladou started become what Bourladou has become. A leader. A boss. A dignitary. A town councilman. Soon a chevalier of the Legion of Honor. He has confided to me, in a tone of delighted embarrassment, that it is going to happen in July. For sure.

"In July? What's happening in July?"

Bourladou silently took hold of the lapel of his jacket and with his thumb performed, upon the buttonhole, an obscene little back and forth movement.

I said, "Say, that's true, you don't have it."

"Flouche is taking care of that."

"Ah, Flouche," I said.

"Yes," said Bourladou, "Flouche."

I know people of all sorts.
They do not measure up to their destinies.

—GUILLAUME APOLLINAIRE

In the course of the same conversation, Bourladou revealed to me that the Erection Committee was going through a difficult time. Doctor Fleuron, its president, had been carried off—as they say—by a stroke. It was too bad: he had had an elderly gentleman's lovely mustache, white and drooping, perfectly presidential.

Chancerel will succeed him. Chancerel is of another style: shoulders, jaw, chest, and character.

"Don't you see," Bourladou says, greatly wrought up, "a communist in the presidency, that simply could not be . . . "

He always knows what can and cannot be. He finds his way effortlessly and unerringly amid mysterious prohibitions and jumbles of initials: S.F.I.O.P.R.L.M.R.P.

"I'll explain it to you . . . "

Bourladou bends toward me, observes me. There shall be no escape; I am in for the initials.

Here they come. The committee has deemed that the presidency belongs to that one among the Resistance organizations which counted the most victims. So they started to enumerate the dead. That's when the tumult began.

"We had five."

"We had seven."

They were soon head over heels into spurious figures and faked additions. They squabbled over corpses. They cheated all they could over the martyrs.

"And our people," Troude shouted, "had eleven of them."

Rave burst out laughing. "Plain horseshit. Eleven? Come on,

you've got to be kidding. Where are you going to dig up eleven from? Let's have a little look at them."

Troude tried digging them up. "There was Credoux," he said. "There was Valache."

"All right," Rave said, "I'll let you have Valache."

"That makes one," the others said. "That makes two. Courtepoint. Balendin. That makes three, four."

"Besançon," Troude said.

At that Rave burst out: "Never for one damned minute was Besançon in with you people."

"He was in the party," Troude yelled.

Those of his party yelled along with him, the rival factions protested, they had themselves a fine shouting match, it was soon bordering on a brawl. They all wanted to take possession of Besançon. He'd been this, no, he'd been that. Before you could say Jack Robinson, Besançon's opinions, words, intentions were recalled, displayed, rattled, interpreted, attested, contested. Impossible to figure out what was what.

However, one could not await any particulars from the concerned party. Besançon, at present, was crushed and rotted flesh. When they extracted him from the mass grave, at the Liberation, the only thing still intact was his bridge—two canines, one incisor. His dentist was called, he recognized the bridge, and thanks to this detail Besançon was identified.

At this point in the discussion, things took a truly serious turn. Some members of the committee claimed that their dead, if not so numerous, outweighed the others through their quality. Soon people in each camp were disparaging the dead of the opposing camp:

"Valache? A curious patriot, that one. In '39 that Valache of yours was pro-Boche . . ."

"At any rate, Valache did not turn his pals in. Whereas Mortimeur . . ."

"Yeah, what about him, what do you have to say about Mortimeur?"

They trundled out old resentments, ill-contained suspicions. The cadavers became questionable. They broke down under the denunciation of the living. They confessed to vanity, foolishness, wiliness, cynical calculation, and contemptible motives.

"And Flampin's execution," shouted Rave. "You're not going to tell me that story was crystal clear . . . "

It was Fauchiez who decided that Flampin had to be eliminated. He said that he had proof. That they were cooked, all of them, if they didn't get rid of that treacherous bastard.

"Seeing as how you've got proof," Caucheron said, "and seeing as how the guys all agree . . . "

"Nobody's forcing you," Fauchiez said.

"Never mind that," Caucheron said, "somebody's got to do it."

Caucheron and Lamoue, using some excuse, got Flampin into a car and drove off with him. The next day, at first light, a roadman discovered Flampin at the bottom of a ditch: two bullets in his head, pockets turned inside out. Neatly done work. The roadman had viewed it as one more act of the sort that meant annoying repercussions for him.

It appeared simple, back in those days, necessary. Later, little by little, doubts surfaced. One came to wonder whether, after all, they hadn't been a bit hasty. Fauchiez's proof hadn't actually been verified by anyone. Fauchiez had ended up in the Buchenwald crematorium. It was recalled that Flampin hadn't been very fond of him. And that for his part he couldn't stand Flampin. Between the two there had been something or other that had to do with women. Something or other about money.

"Yes," Bourladou repeats, "you'll grant me that it's disturbing."

For Caucheron as well it must be disturbing. The others—

Lamoue, Fauchiez—are dead. But he's still alive, he's still here, in the little hairdresser's salon he has on the rue aux Choux. Through the window, underneath the inscription *Hair Dresser* in white letters, you see his long clerical figure. He is waiting for customers. He is watching the goings-on in the rue aux Choux, where nothing is going on.

"Your thoughts seem to be elsewhere," Bourladou worries.

"I am thinking about Caucheron," I say.

Caucheron is a man of forty, a gray-haired and solitary man. He expresses himself in the way valets do in turn-of-the-century novels: "Shall I give Monsieur a scalp massage? Does Monsieur desire a splash of lavender water?"

He's the man who killed Flampin. When he arranges the towel around my neck, on my skin I feel his hands, which are dry and cold. Bad circulation probably. I say to myself that he killed Flampin with those same hands.

"Funny guy, doesn't talk much," Bourladou observes. "Curious, actually, for a hairdresser."

More than once, while Caucheron's scissors were clicking insectlike in my hair, I tried to picture the scene. Not the murder; the part that came before. Before is the hardest. When everything is set, when the act has already snapped shut around you, leaving you caught, although nothing has yet been accomplished.

I visualize the scene in some sleepy little café. Lamoue and Caucheron are waiting. Lamoue has his everyday look, he's cleaning his fingernails, and with his eyes of a white rabbit he's watching two railway employees playing a card game.

And how about me, Caucheron wonders, do I have my everyday look? He buries his hands in his pockets, for they are shaking: here I go, about to screw up.

Flampin has come in. He has shaken his wet raincoat. He has said something to the woman who owns the café, and she has laughed. He has petted a large cat that lay asleep on the telephone directory.

"You aren't much bothered by the restrictions, are you now?"

There were the cardplayers in their loosened tunics and their caps pushed back on their heads. There was that woman who was saying: "For vegetables it isn't too bad, I manage, the problem is meat . . . "

Flampin knows everybody. He gives a friendly greeting to the cardplayers. As he passes by he gives a thump to the old man reading the personals in the newspaper: "Love life still going strong?"

That's the kind of fellow he was, a straightforward guy. He was well liked, with that worthy face of his, his red-cheeked and heavy-jowled face of a middle-aged shopkeeper.

He asked Caucheron: "Why are you looking at me like that?"

"No reason," Caucheron said. "I'm just looking at you."

Bourladou is splashing about in a welter of explanations. He has now got to where Chancerel stepped in. Chancerel's eloquence was able to calm the committee's passions. Bourladou reconstitutes his speech, strikes poses, thunders: "The mystique of the Resistance, comrades, was not an empty expression . . . "

But it's Flampin's voice I am continuing to listen to . . . Flampin is relating how he found shirts on the black market, synthetic and cotton, they're worth what they're worth, mustn't be choosy in times like these.

And Caucheron is looking at him. From close up he can see the freckles on his face, the pimples, the little veins over his cheekbones. He can see the little line of dried blood near his lip: Flampin cut himself while shaving. Because of that silly little scratch, Flampin suddenly strikes him as vulnerable, naive, defenseless. From afar, in advance, the business seems clear, almost easy. Someone or other says: "Okay, somebody's got to do it." But now Caucheron is in front of Flampin, breathing Flampin's odor. He recognizes Flampin's cologne—Houbigant. He is inside the cloud of hearty good humor Flampin gives out:

"I'm not in favor of depriving oneself, life's too short for that."
Caucheron sees the little scratch. He sees a clumsy, boastful,
unsuspecting man. He repeats to himself: a bastard . . . he's a
bloody-handed bastard . . . Fauchiez says that he has evidence.
But he looks at the little scratch, and he's not sure of anything
anymore.

A quarter of an hour. It will have lasted a quarter of an hour.
Afterward, you have your whole life to remember it. When he
is standing behind his shop window, gazing emptily toward the
street, it may be of Flampin's little scratch that Caucheron is
thinking. Or he might not be thinking of anything—people do
less thinking than one believes, and it's just as well for them.

"The communists voted against him," says Bourladou.

"Against whom?"

"Why, against Chancerel—come on now, I'm talking about
Chancerel."

Bourladou darts a suspicious glance at me. "Needless to say,"
I hastily stammer, "right, the communists . . . "

And so it was that, despite communist opposition, Chancerel
was elected president of the Erection Committee. Thus was the
crisis resolved and, according to Bourladou, one could not wish
for a happier conclusion to this conflict of the living among
themselves and of the living with the dead.

The living become presidents. The dead become monuments. The monument once solidly planted on the ground,
together with its palm branches, its stacked weapons and its
moldings, the living have no more questions to put to the dead.
They give up seeking their truth within the confusion of deeds
and words, dreams and roles. That's what justifies the existence
of monuments to the dead: they place a check upon curiosities.

"Good God, but it's freezing in this place of yours," Bourladou
suddenly remarks.

I offer a pitiful excuse: "The stove has been drawing poorly for some time, I don't know what the matter is . . . "

"Hmph, hmph," Bourladou goes.

He seizes the poker and attacks the coal—*hmph hmph*—with brisk violence. A few hiccups, a little smoke, and the stove is going merrily. "There you are," says Bourladou, very proud of himself.

Yes indeed, he is successful in his every undertaking. He paces back and forth through the room, halts in front of the Unknown Soldier, sings:

Le soldat est comme son pompon,
Plus il devient vieux, plus il devient con.

Would he not be about to come out with his ritual joke apropos of Iseult, whose heavy masculine tread is now resounding through the wall? No; on my table he has discovered *The Lady at the Claridge*, in the "Mystery" series. A novel that Porcher lent to me.

"You absolutely have to read this," Porcher told me.

Absolutely: that's one of his words. Porcher has that peremptory style, and that habit of imposing his pleasures on others. I offered a little resistance: "Detective stories, you know, I—"

"This one," Porcher told me, "is a classic."

Fine, I took *The Lady at the Claridge*. On the cover is a femme fatale in an apple-green dress. She is conversing with a beefy fellow in a rakishly cocked fedora.

"You'll observe," Porcher explained to me, "they read this or that, depends on their taste. You've got a taste, romantic is what they want, poetic. Or else dirty books. Or else deep stuff, Sartre, Paul Bourget, if you see what I mean. But detective stories, everybody goes for them, that's something you'll observe. Even intellectuals, even professors. Everybody. It's a need, in our age."

Bourladou spends a long moment leafing through *The Lady*

at the Claridge, produces a few "hmph, hmphs" fraught with meaning, and finally asks me as he tosses the volume aside: "And how about you, making any progress with that book of yours? Pleased with the way it's going?"

He's beginning to annoy me with this stuff. I look at the apple-green lady and the beefy guy. Do I have what it takes to write a book? Even a book like *The Lady at the Claridge?*

Almost all the people I have known have rung false.

Spent an hour with Dardillot. He found himself on the wrong side during the Occupation—among those who lacked courage and a sense of the opportune. They say his opinions scandalized his compatriots. I wouldn't have believed that of Dardillot. I took him for a harmless old fellow and a drunkard, but I never suspected that he was without national feeling. The speeches he used to make, notably about the army and the country, struck me as appropriate and even—so far as I was concerned—edifying. I imagine that he was out to shock a few of the habitués at the Trois Colonnes; but there are some subjects about which we do not joke.

I came upon him as, furtive and hobbling, he was slinking out of a bistro. I shook hands with him. Rather mechanically, but the gesture moved him, though he tried not to show it.

"Hadn't you better mind what you are about, young man? You're not worried about compromising yourself?"

With that he let out a gurgling laugh. "A dirty bastard, my dear boy, you're shaking the hand of a dirty bastard."

He said it swaggeringly, but with the scared look in his eyes old paupers and street peddlers have. He had become downright hideous: yellowed mustache, nose unwiped, that pince-nez sitting askew.

"You see, my boy, old Dardillot's a man one no longer lifts his hat to. No lifting of hats to bastards."

He gestured broadly with one wavering hand, designating the town. The town where every virtuous hand refused his hand, where no honest hat was raised when he went by.

"Why yes, they all came to the decision together, the patriots, the good citizens, the certified resisters, the handshake experts, the hat-lifting specialists, all in agreement on the matter, my dear boy, unanimous: Dardillot, Horace (a preposterous first name, I grant you), Horace Dardillot, onetime soldier in the Great War, onetime university agrégé, no longer has the right to any outward signs of his countrymen's respect. Into the garbage can with old Dardillot."

He pushed me in the direction of the bistro he had just left, the while repeating: "Into the garbage can, into the garbage can."

We sat in a deserted little room that smelled of laundry and bleach: three tables, an enameled stove, a yellow cat on the stove and an old woman in a corner. She had laid aside some ragged old clothes she had been mending in order to bring us glasses of Pernod. The old woman is deaf and no longer sound of mind. "I'm her only customer," Dardillot told me, his index finger raised. "A serious customer. Yuh."

I recognized the grumbling sound with which he used to punctuate his corrections of our Latin versions in the eighth grade. "The entire crowd, *omnis multitudo*, nominative, clamors in unison, *conclamat*, the entire crowd clamors in unison, yuh . . ."

Dardillot took a drink, wiped his mustache with his hand, belched. "I am fond of this place," he told me. "Just the kind of place that befits a solitary and dishonored old age."

I made no reply, I don't see what I could have replied.

He went on: "Philoctetes . . . You remember Philoctetes? No, of course not. A lad they left to rot away on an island. The Greeks, exactly. Well, right now I'm like Philoctetes: the decayed tooth that's been yanked from the community . . . My dear boy, this, right here, is Philoctetes' island. My only refuge . . . "

Pointing to them one by one, his gesture had brought together the three tables, the stove, the old woman, the posters on the wall advertising Martini, Cap Corse. He declaimed: "This shelter for a day wherein death to await."

And he added, suddenly become perfectly simple: "This is surely where I'll croak. Here with the cat and the old woman." Long silence. His face deeply furrowed, his chin drooping, Dardillot contemplated his death with a bitter satisfaction. Then he drank from his glass and belched. Then he removed his pince-nez and, clasping it between thumb and index finger, shook it before my nose:

"Think, dear boy, think about the estimable figure I might have become in my old age. Better than estimable: imposing. That's the word: an imposing old gentleman, all his wrinkles just where they belong, his jowls hung aright, a stately presence. That's right: dignity and presence. A hint of unction. Remarks carefully groomed . . . The personage with the university background, you know, positioned midway between the old magistrate and the old priest. Portly, gray, grave . . . They'd have said: 'Monsieur Dardillot, ah, a very distinguished mind, a humanist . . . ' Yuh. I would have played my role amid the other old gentlemen. Bridge with retired colonels, engineers from the Department of Civil Engineering. Belonged to the local bibliophiles' society, the Folklore Studies Club. Rubbed elbows with the departmental archivist and Canon Coudérouille . . . Let's drop the subject."

His gurgling laughter died off into clearings of the throat, some uncontrolled coughing, hiccups. Having got his breath back, he intoned a few words in a clownish singsong:

It's over, faded dream, visions vanished and gone.

He stuck his pince-nez back on his swollen nose. He stared for some time at the festooned curtain dangling from a rod against the windowed door of the tavern. On the other side was the town, with its colonels, its canons, its book lovers. And all of a sudden Dardillot flew into a rage.

"They can all go fuck themselves," he shouted. "Don't need the esteem of those goddamned cocos . . ."

Becoming calmer: "Fools, my boy, simpletons. Simpletons or scoundrels. I know them well, you can bet you. Fifty years! I've spent fifty years in this sewer of their shopkeepers' passions. I know every bloody thing they have in their heads, in their hearts, in their bellies. I know what they've got in their pockets and in their beds. The stories I could tell, there's no end to them, do believe me. Stories about all of them. About Flouche, for instance, that great man of theirs. About your friend Bourladou, a prize ninny, that one . . ."

Relaxed, familiar, mocking: "At present, you understand, I have some perspective on all this, I'm no longer in the dance, that enables me to see things more clearly. Now it's my turn to summon them to appear. I bring them in one by one, I have them march past, just the way draftees are made to do before a medical board. Strip, gentleman, let's have a little look at what's hiding underneath your solid citizen's costume. I weigh them, measure them, evaluate them, turn them around. Okay, the next one. Well, my dear friend, grotesque is what they are. Sickening. And it's they who dabble in the assignment of reputations. They are the Just, the Administrators of Justice. The equals of God, experts in good and evil. Laughable, wouldn't you say?

He wasn't laughing at all. His ruined face now expressed only fatigue. "Pay no attention," he groaned, "a little outburst. I take on like this from time to time."

The yellow cat, now awake, jumped down cautiously from its stove and rubbed against our legs. Dardillot picked it up and placed it on his lap.

"A little outburst," he repeated. "It still gets to me. It takes a while, you understand, to accustom yourself to abjection. At the beginning, you stifle, you struggle. But I'll get used to it, don't you worry, I'll get used to it . . . "

He was stroking the cat absently. I told him that things weren't as bad as he made out, and that it was generally allowed that he had done nothing really serious.

"Don't you believe a word of it," he said to me.

He tossed the yellow cat to the floor and, meowing, it sought refuge in the old lady's petticoats.

"Not one word. No one would take it into his head to question my status as a dirty bastard. It's official, my dear boy. I've got my last name and my first name on the list of dirty bastards. What more do you want? A list, that's not open to discussion. Nope."

He had resumed the sententious tone of a longtime pedagogue. He articulated his sentences unhurriedly:

"You understand, on emerging from a time of violent and ambiguous events you find yourself amid total confusion. No one is certain of having been at all times beyond reproach. This creates a malaise. A threat to the community's moral equilibrium. So the list of dirty bastards is drawn up in haste. You've got to have it. There has to be a list of dirty bastards in order that those who aren't on the list be assured of the correctness of their principles and the steadfastness of their conduct. The dirty bastards once identified, registered, labeled, and consigned to abjection, the community feels itself pure. A community, a town, needs to feel itself pure. Just take a look at ours. Ever since the census of dirty bastards was taken, we have been swimming in a state of epic excitement."

As if looking past the little curtain hanging over the door, Dardillot's gaze seemed to be detailing an invisible upwelling of heroism.

"A proud town, let me tell you . . . "

A weak gurgle of laughter.

"Ha, the stories they must have cranked out for you—those false identity papers, those parachutists. I did this, I did that; me me me. Funks they assuredly are not, these compatriots of yours. No sir. In this town of theirs a man's a man. He's got guts, and heart. Old French blood. And balls. All the anatomical features of energy. Yuh."

A moment of dismal coughing. Bringing up closer to me an irritated face on which his pince-nez was quivering:

"Note how even my language is deteriorating—curious, no? My vocabulary has become sloppy. I'm coming apart everywhere, my boy. I'm decomposing. That's what they lead to, prison, Pernod, and public scorn. What those things have been able to make your professor of belles lettres into . . . "

Some more of his heavy, dismal coughing.

"A learned man, a scholar . . . Titles to which no one challenged my right, monsieur. Consider that in another time I published an essay on Jules de Rességuier. Three hundred pages, and nicely composed, by God—they'd still be found in the municipal library were anyone to take the trouble to look for them . . . "

While I was paying the old woman, who took an eternity figuring out my change, Dardillot, planted in the center of the room, facing the town, was declaiming:

Ses malheurs n'avaient point abattu sa fierté.

Outside, he said abruptly: "You take me for a drunk, don't you? Yes, yes, you do, it doesn't matter. It's what they all say: an old drunk. Well, between the two of us, I'm not even that. You hear? Not even a real drunk. I'm a failure at everything."

He pointed a dogmatic finger at me: "In the novels of . . . what's his name? That Russian . . . Anyway, that's where you see what a true drunk is like. The guy, you know, who creeps around on his knees, who pounds his stomach with his fists, who hollers magnificent things . . . That's the way it should be done. You picture the scene, right? Dardillot appearing at the stroke of six o'clock at the Café des Trois Colonnes, in the midst of the Just . . . I'd roll at their feet, among the tables. I'd crawl. I'd weep, stammer, it would be awful. I would talk to them about the soul, about sin. And they'd be ashamed, my dear boy, they'd be ashamed of themselves, and of me . . . "

He started to hobble off into the darkness. After having taken a few steps, he turned and shouted in my direction: "You know how it will end. In the company of the cat and the old woman, remember that. Between the cat and the old woman."

Dardillot dreams of himself as a hero out of Dostoevsky. But try as he may to play the insulted and the injured, he'll never amount to more than an embittered and tedious gentleman, a petty boozer mired in the monologues of an erstwhile schoolteacher.

I thought about him skimming through *The Lady at the Claridge*. I take Porcher's book with me when I go to the restaurant. I set it beside my plate. It doesn't interest me much, but it protects me against the initiatives of overly sociable neighbors.

That day it is a youth with a humid pink face who has installed himself opposite me: "You'll allow me?"

His voice announced liveliness, sociability, optimism, self-confidence. You must watch out for these joyful lads. They are full of opinions. They know what to think about different makes of cars, wines, dead languages, bicycle races, government crises.

I studiously turn the pages of *The Lady at the Claridge*. I decorticate the prawns, I chew the breaded cutlet they serve at the Restaurant de l'Epine d'Or, Croquedale proprietor, plain cooking. The essential thing is not to look up: the guy is lying in wait for me. The slightest weakness on my part and I'll meet his gaze sunk in blue jelly. And that would suffice. The guy would politely formulate an opinion about something. It would be necessary to reply. And all his opinions would file out one after the other.

I keep reading, my nose in my book, my mouth full of food.

The story is about a lady dancer who has been murdered. Who could have done it? I try to guess, give up; finally I start thinking about the one murderer I know personally: a certain Sidère, one of my classmates in grade school.

This fellow killed a milliner—by means of a razor, and rather clumsily, moreover. The deed once done, his identity papers in his pocket, he betook himself to the local police and turned himself in. That won him ten years in the prison of those days, and the commentaries of the regional press. Sidère is a pudgy boy, with whitish skin and with very little to say. I don't see what could be done with him in a detective novel.

To become a character in a novel presupposes aptitudes, qualities. Sidère didn't have what it takes. With guys like him it's over with right away. You never move beyond the anecdote; you do not attain the novel.

It's more or less Dardillot's case: he doesn't have what it takes either. Lots of people like that. Spongy, mushy existences, within which the incident sinks and rots.

A further example is provided to me by Madame Corchetuile, the butcher's wife. Her husband let himself be whisked away by a dumpy little lady. During the first days, customers streamed into the shop to see how Madame Corchetuile was taking this disgrace. They found the butcher's wife ready for business behind the counter, her mouth in the shape of an ace of hearts and frozen in an unalterable smile. Truly quite as ever, neither uncomfortable nor concerned:

"He'll come home, sure, don't you worry, once he's had enough of it . . . "

Corchetuile did indeed come home at the end of three weeks, rather shamefaced. He resumed his commercial habits, his conjugal habits. When on Sundays the Corchetuiles come rolling out from eleven o'clock mass, placid, prosperous, innocent as two cucumbers, you are made to realize that upon natures of that sort the procedures of novelese have no effect.

Neither, I'm sure, do they work upon this boy with the big tender cheeks. Nor upon any whomsoever of the diners at L'Epine d'Or: you need but observe the gravity with which they consume their Melun brie or their rice pudding—one glance settles the matter. Our *romanesque* fails to sink its teeth into the Epine d'Or clientele.

Mediocre, halfway-alive beings, incapable of giving any depth to their lives. Powerless to impose on adversity the richness and intensity of an adventure; on chance, the shape of a destiny.

There's chance and misfortune enough for everybody. That's not what's lacking. The important thing is not that something happen to somebody, but that somebody make something out of what happens to him. There must be someone at the finish line. Someone vulnerable and ingenious, open to experience, and complicated.

Preferably somebody with leisure and private income. The *romanesque* is a privilege of the fashionable, a luxury. The novel, in our tradition, transpires at the Guermantes'. Not in the space particular to clerks and the keepers of public squares. Not in Porcher's neighborhood, in Iseult's, not among one-legged men on their benches and women doing their laundry.

"The marquise requested her carriage and went out at five o'clock . . . " The old boy had it straight; he didn't say the cleaning lady or the salesgirl at Monoprix. When the marquise goes out, we are assured that her heart and her flesh are quivering with the most exquisite virtualities. But the cleaning lady is only heading toward her mops and buckets of dirty water. Or else, she is going out to buy supplies in the neighborhood. She hurries along because the milk store will soon close. She is thinking about the price of carrots or sardines. That can't even be called *going out*. It is as though she were sewn up inside her cleaning woman's condition.

It is in the finer neighborhoods that they are able to treat themselves to savory pangs of conscience, rich slices of sin, well-done remorse; give themselves over to violences that satisfy the imagination; cultivate sorrow, revolt, courage, cowardice, to these common postures imparting the character of gratuitousness, unexpectedness, and complexity, which are the very essence of novelese.

Merely park them on a stool inside a metro gate, these duchesses out of Marcel Proust or Balzac, merely get them punching holes in bits of cardboard for an eight-hour-a-day stretch and every day, Monday through Saturday, and you'll see what remains of their distinguished dramas. All there will be left to describe is fatigue and varicose veins, gas bills to pay and waits in line to speak to someone at city hall. Not very *romanesque*, any of that. Life is short on the *romanesque* when you have to earn a living.

Life reduces itself to this slogging on step by step, day by day, dime by dime, hardship by hardship. It becomes strung out, it unravels, it hangs in tatters everywhere. Without beginning, or end, or shape. The likes of us have no great dramas. We have nothing but troubles, hassles. And barely the time to think about them. Because our time crumbles away in absurd toil and sordid calculations. Through this all we wend our way, mind focused on the immediate worry, and after this one there will be others. Always a chore to finish, kids to wipe, bills to pay. And the fear of being late. The inflexible hours of the factory and the office. Limitations evident everywhere. No freedom, no play. Poor people have no influence upon the outcome of things. They are trapped within it. And when events single them out, they surrender to them, moaning and complaining.

Sometimes I do get the urge to actually write the book that Bourladou believes I am writing. At such times I look at the photographs on the walls of my room. These unknown persons' stories—it seems to me I am able to tell what they are.

This tempts me for a moment. But I give up: they don't even have what you could call a story. You don't put together a story out of tales of military service or hospitalizations, of the youngster's whooping cough, the price of potatoes, or the size of an unemployment check. Monotonous and stagnant daily defeat isn't a story . . .

Of all literary impostures, the populist variety strikes me as the most indecent, feigning to believe that the poor buggers (the humble, to speak in the compassionate style) possess an inner life, appreciable spiritual riches, unexplored complexities.

No place for the humble in the novel. No more place than in the bars on the Champs-Elysées.

The man who works does not come within the province of the novel; he comes within that of psychotechnics. You summon him to a laboratory. White-smocked assistants place him in front of pieces of machinery. He presses buttons. He manipulates thingamajigs in wood or steel. He watches lights come on and go off. There are devices that register his mistakes, devices that are never wrong. Thanks to these devices, the man is evaluated. His memory, his attention, his aptitudes, his reflexes. All that is converted into figures. The figures are written down, a graph is generated—a psychological profile, as they say. And everything worth knowing about his inner life is there, in abscissas and ordinates. One glance at the graph, no more is needed. You see what the man can do, and what can be done with him.

Make him into a bus driver or an accountant. A human tool, in any case. And who presents about as many novelistic possibilities as a drill press or a monkey wrench.

Absence of an inner life. Or else the inner life stamped out by daily living . . . When I assemble my experience of individuals, I always run up against that alternative. Either the eaters at

Croquedale's restaurant, the readers of *Figaro*, the talkers at the Trois Colonnes, the erectors of monuments to the dead, the detectors of rumors going around. Or else the Crabs.

This is probably the right point to transcribe the remarks I overheard the other evening at the Trois Colonnes, and which concern the life, the death, and the posthumous situation of Marécasse.

I made my way into a fog of laughter, voices, and tobacco smoke. Inside all that floated the owner, flaccid. He is called Monsieur Louis. Bald, pug-nosed, and with his sorrowful mustache, he looks like an old boarding-school master or a clerk in a pawnshop.

The owner's wife, at the cash register, was busy repairing torn hundred-franc notes with the help of a roll of gummed paper tape.

"Filthy weather," Monsieur Louis said to me. "This drizzle, it's worse than real rain. Weather for catching a cold and stuff like that, for sure."

The waiter asked me what it would be. I answered that it would be a glass of sweet vermouth. "Like for someone sick," the waiter said.

Around me, Business, Government Service, Industry, and the Liberal Professions were having themselves games of cards and aperitifs. At the adjoining table I recognized Couvreur, Scie (of Scie, Incorporated), Rudognon, the bookstore owner in the rue Douillet. The three were talking about the decision to close down the country's brothels. They held this measure to be an unfortunate one, from the moral viewpoint and from the viewpoint of hygiene as well.

"Statistics have established," Rudognon revealed, "that since they've been shut down, the spread of venereal diseases has taken on alarming proportions."

He sipped some pink liquid and reiterated it very heatedly: "Alarming."

An old man was reading the papers. Elderly, scrawny, and goateed: Grandfather Vane, the stenography teacher. Quiet as could be in his little corner, where he sat every evening.

The Batrachian was in his place as well. Hunched over on the moleskin-covered banquette, his eyes bleak, his cheeks lifeless, spots of Pernod on his vest. They say that once upon a time he was into literature: he had written poems, at a later point novels. Anyhow, he had become a kind of batrachian who from between his dentures would grind out recollections of Pierre Veber and Alfred Capus.

All the Habitués were in their places. The old ones, the faithful, the unshakable. Those you always see there. Who have ceased to change, who have lost all desire to change their place or their life. They have taken their definitive form. They have found the place and the formula.

I admire, as I drink my sweet vermouth, these static, fulfilled, untroubled existences. They're lucky devils, the Habitués. Habituated to everything: to themselves, the world, to other Habitués. In such an existence they no longer find anything surprising, they are not bothered by it, it does not disgust them.

In aging some have become gray, others have become red. An Habitué either dries up, becomes ligneous, mildewed; or else he swells, becomes pulpy and florid, takes on an amplitude, a radiance. Scie, of Scie, Incorporated, belongs to the ashen, tense variety. Couvreur, to the rubescent variety.

I hear Couvreur's voice: "Talking about whorehouses, do you remember the time when Barbeterre . . . "

The waiter lolls from table to table, dishcloth in his fist. And so what's it going to be for these gentlemen here? Two café-crèmes, two. There you go.

"They recognized his Talbot, which he had left parked in

front of number twelve," Couvreur says. "So, just to play a little joke on him . . . "

Bourladou appears. He comes on in wearing a pleasant-looking informal overcoat. On either side, most cordially, he pats Habitués' shoulders. From afar he flings little smiles and nods toward Business, Industry, Government Service, and the Liberal Professions, who send smiles and nods back to him. You would think a dozen Bourladous were greeting Bourladou who is greeting them. At length he gets to where I am.

"I'm late," he explains to me, drawing his thick hands out of the fur-lined gloves sheathing them. "I was held up at the Erection Committee."

"When Barbeterre left the cathouse," Couvreur says, "and there was no sign of his jalopy . . . "

The waiter shows up and inquires what it will be for Bourladou. Well now, I do believe, yes, it'll be a little glass of port.

"Like for someone sick," the waiter goes.

"Were you talking about Barbeterre?" Bourladou asks the Habitués at the next table. "Ah now, there's one for you, that Barbeterre, he had hold of life by the right end."

"I was telling about the time," Couvreur says, "when he thought that somebody had swiped his jalopy when he was at number twelve . . . "

"He walked straight to the police station to file a complaint," Bourladou says. "Naturally, we'd let the police chief in on the joke."

The Habitués laugh. The Habitués' laughter derives from the hiccup, from the bark, from the asthma attack . . . It terminates in sniffles and rumblings. I join timidly in this powerful music, but I have no natural disposition toward collective hilarity.

Bourladou is moaning, tears in his eyes: "That rascal Barbeterre, that rascal Barbeterre . . . " Then he turns toward me, stubs out his cigarette in the Dubonnet ashtray, and leans forward, his elbows on the table: "Yes, can you imagine, there was a squabble in the committee, it was over Marécasse."

The stub does not want to expire. It smokes and stinks. It stubbornly persists. All by itself among the other stubs, shriveled, yellow, resigned, completely dead.

"Marécasse," I say, "isn't he the one who was deported?"

"Precisely," Bourladou says, "to Dachau, where he died. The question this raises . . . "

At last, the stub is dead. Dry and dead like the other stubs, lying within a small disorder of ashes and matches.

"This raises the question," Bourladou goes on, "of knowing whether he is entitled . . . "

"And Barbeterre's funeral, you remember Barbeterre's funeral?"

Monsieur Louis, who had been floating nearby, came over to hear Rudognon evoke once again how, during Barbeterre's funeral service, when the congregation were going up to the altar for the offertory, Rocher used this opportunity to switch around the hats left behind on the chairs.

"And I can still see," says the weeping Rudognon, "I can still see Rougagnol's face when we were all out of there and he was putting a little brown velvet hat on his head."

"And the Chief Magistrate of the Court in a schoolboy's cap."

"And Captain Viorne in a bowler . . . "

"Mickey's bowler," Bourladou breaks in. "Remember? Mickey was what we used to call Sardoine. Sardoine the solicitor. A hard man to get on with, a sourpuss. He was fit to be tied that day . . . "

They laugh some more. That rascal Barbeterre. They're happy to be laughing together. To be laughing about the same things. To achieve communion through whooping it up together. To feel themselves identical and as one. Similarly amused by the same gags, warmed up by the same remarks. While they may not all be of the same opinion, they all have the same way of not being of the same opinion.

"Now, where were we?" Bourladou says. "Ah yes, I was talking to you about Marécasse. Well, the question facing the committee is to find out whether Marécasse will have his name on the monument. In a sense, he has the right to have it there. I can buy that. Here's a guy who died in Dachau. A monument is raised, you put his name with the others, it looks logical."

"Yes," I say, "it does."

"Just wait a minute," Bourladou rejoins. "Insofar as he's dead, he has the right, I grant you that. You'll get no argument from me there. But follow me carefully now: His name on the memorial, now what does that mean? It means that Marécasse was a Resister. Now, that—I don't accept it. I said that to the committee. Having decided that resistance is the matter at hand, Marécasse, dead or not dead, has nothing to do with it."

"You're saying Marécasse wasn't in the Resistance?"

"Come on now," exclaims Bourladou, bubbling over with merriment, "you knew him, you can't really believe that Marécasse . . ."

I did know him. I attempt to recall to myself what he was like. It's difficult: such a furtive creature, so colorless. Sort of overweight, it seems to me. Sort of fair-haired, low-slung. But he gets away from me. His face dissolves just as I seem to have gotten hold of some of its features. His face is absorbed, nullified by the overspreading reality of the Café des Trois Colonnes. People go out, come in, produce laughter, smoke, words. How much does that come to, waiter? No, don't worry about it, this round's on me. No room for Marécasse's ridiculous shade in all this living matter. It's too bulky, too compact, all this, too full of flesh and heat, it weighs too much. Marécasse isn't forcible. But from such an unobtrusive individual you couldn't expect a very self-asserting ghost. He isn't insistent. "Scared of his own shadow," Bourladou declares to me. "The sort of gentleman who is unwilling to compromise himself, who does nothing but mind his own business, who keeps his ass covered, who tries to keep out of sight." Bourladou shrugs and blows some of his contemptuous *hmph*s from his nose.

"Great chassis," observes Couvreur from near where we are sitting.

With a connoisseur's eye he is scrutinizing a woman who has just walked in. Rudognon looks at the woman and clucks. He pokes Scie with his elbow. Scie's clucking joins his. A light stir spreads among the Habitués, something like a gust that briefly sets the pear tree's leaves and the laundry on the fence to fluttering. Even the cardplayers' gestures seem to hesitate ever so slightly. Grandfather Vane's goatee emerges from the newspapers whence he extracts his daily ration of rapes, of abortions, and of human debris in shoe boxes.

"That little gal's nicely put together," Bourladou murmurs.

He smiles over the memories that glide past within his private universe.

In the depths of a fog, the faces of the Habitués, multiplied by the mirrors, oscillate back and forth, red, gray, red, gray. Bourladou proposes that we have another vermouth. Come on, come on, just let me take care of it. At the neighboring table, the gasoline tax is the subject under discussion now. Same again, waiter. You got it, the waiter cries.

"But," I say, "there had to be some reason or other why Marécasse was sent to Dachau."

"Marécasse? Not at all. Somebody said something about him to the Gestapo, that's all it took. You mustn't think the Boches were all that particular. One more or one less. They tossed him in along with some others they had, and there he was: shipped off, liquidated, whappo. Gone."

With a flick of the wrist, performed a little above the ashtray, Bourladou represents the fate of that glassy-eyed victim. Whappo. Gone. That's that.

"But, look here, whoever would have wanted to turn him in?"

"That's a pretty long story," Bourladou says.

He finds it surprising that I am not in the know. "It's true you're not in the know about anything. Well, just listen a bit, you'll find it interesting."

The Habitués at the neighboring table, who also find it interesting, turn happy faces toward us. The problem of taxes on fuel will wait.

"Now of course," Bourladou begins, "you know nothing about things that are known to everyone: that during the Occupation Marécasse's wife was sleeping with a German, yes, old friend, with a German veterinarian."

"A handsome fellow," Rudognon puts in. The others agree: a well-built fellow, a real muscle man, must have been around six and a half feet tall, huge shoulders. Whereas it had to be said that Marécasse was not very well favored. Squat, with no build at all, really lousy-looking and not very smart. A woman like Marécasse's wife, you can understand that she needed compensations. Discreet and restrained laughter from the Habitués. The adulterous wife's physical appearance is then lingeringly analyzed. Not precisely pretty, no, but exciting. Gorgeous legs. "Peen-up," lets out the enraptured Scie of Scie, Incorporated. Slightly on the thin side according to Bourladou, who appreciates richly made women. (Like the little gal over there, take that one for instance, that girl's nicely put together.) But anyway, to get back to Marécasse's wife, the thing above all was she knew how to deck herself out. Elegant, that she was. Peen-up. Whatever, a slut of the first water. That she took lovers, all right. It was normal, it was even moral, with the husband she had. But males, good God, you can find them elsewhere than in the Wehrmacht, can't you? In the very middle of the war. A Boche. Getting herself fucked by a Boche. The Habitués' indignation bursts forth confusedly, flares up a second time, and subsides into virtuous and sorrowful utterances.

"You can guess what happens after that," Bourladou says.

"What happens after that?"

"Why yes, he's informed on."

"It would have been Madame Marécasse . . . "

"Who else would you have it be?" says Bourladou.

"And," I say, "we are sure of that?"

"Sure?" Bourladou goes. "Sure? In these hugger-muggeries you're never sure of anything. But think about it . . . "

This is the time when, one by one, the Habitués (it's already half past, got to run, my wife's waiting for me) stand up blowing and puffing, pull down the points of their vests, button their second button, and, stooped over and arms flailing, struggle into their coats. They carefully augment their bulk with articles made of felt, knitted wool, leather, suede, woven wool, silk, and rabbit fur.

"Think about it a bit," Bourladou tells me.

The spouses are waiting in the recesses of abysmal abodes. Soups are waiting in familial serving bowls, and steam while they wait.

"Nobody had anything against him, against Marécasse . . . "

Bourladou explains the situation to me, unhurriedly, one elbow on the table, a hand on his thigh. Unhurriedly, patiently. With one may presumes and from this I deducts. Couvreur, Scie, and Rudognon nod their agreement. Yes, that's how they see the affair, that surely is the way things happened.

The Batrachian raps a spoon against the edge of his saucer, to draw the waiter's attention. You've got it. Nobody had anything against Marécasse. An accommodating husband, not encumbering, loath to make a fuss. The Batrachian leaves. Grandfather Vane leaves. On the way out he exchanges a few remarks with Monsieur Louis about dry cold and about damp cold, by some preferred to dry cold.

"The two of them dream the thing up together, you understand. You see the veterinarian saying, 'Don't you think, honey,

that would do him good, a nice little trip to a foreign country?'
And you see her answering, 'Sure, honey, it'll give him something new to think about . . . '"

Mirthful gruntings from Scie, Couvreur, and Rudognon. We have a sense of humor. And a moral sense, too. Noble sentiments. We're not rotten bastards, not us, like that Boche and that slut.

"And so there you have it," Bourladou concludes.

He finishes his glass of port: there you have it. Marécasse is dead. He was not entitled to his death—an inadvertence on the part of destiny, an error in accounting. Not one whit of it did he understand. But one does not often understand why one dies; or why one lives.

Scie, of Scie, Incorporated, blithely notes that in an age like our own you do indeed behold some curious things. Yes indeed, say the others, that's very true. I say so too. And there we are, in good standing with philosophy.

A curious age and curious things. Words ready to hand, ready-made, familiar, worn out, and inconsequential. Words that simulate thought and that keep you from thinking. Were one to think what one speaks, where would that lead us?

We become habituated to ages and to things. With the Habitués, the tragic and the absurd no longer sink in. What's essential is to live. To be on the right side, the side of the living. On the side with the port wine, the peen-up girls, the Trois Colonnes. The Habitués dreamily savor all this unctuous life, which fills their bellies, their balls, their brains. All this life plunged in a limitless welter of life. There are in our country at least one hundred thousand Cafés des Trois Colonnes. We are in the Café of the Three Hundred Thousand Columns. In here we are two million Habitués. Or maybe twenty million. The party of the Living. Two million craniums with brains inside, and in the brains opinions about the price of gasoline and the housing question. Four million cerebral hemispheres. Four million testicles. Four million meters of large intestine. Sixteen million meters of small intestine. Sixteen thousand, twenty thousand miles of entrails. Taken together, the Habitués make quite a pile. They take up a lot of space. Without counting the Habitués' wives. Or the Habitués' children, who will become habituated in their turn, even before they come of age. A dead man is of hardly any weight against so much existence. Above all a dead man like Marécasse. Not even a hero. Not even a dead man whose death was according to Hoyle. An unusable dead man. Who sneaked into death with false papers. A stowaway. A guy who isn't in his place and who wonders what the hell he's doing where he is. And who says to himself surely must be a reason, but which one, for God's sake, which one?

"In the end," Bourladou recounts, "I told them at the committee—my blood was up, you know, I may have gone too far—I just came out and told them that we had to get it straight between us whether it was a monument to the Resisters we wanted to put up, or was it a monument to cuckolds?"

He laughs, emits his "hmph hmph" a few times, fools with his wallet. The Trois Colonnes is by now almost deserted. As one by one the men withdraw it is turning into an impoverished place, a scene of devastation. Still a half-dozen of the living amid the dirty tables and the shoved-about chairs. I look at the vapor on the windows. I feel weary and bitter. Bourladou's voice envelops me:

"I don't blame anything on Marécasse. I even feel badly because of him. What else can I say to you? Just that, if he were able to express his opinion, I am certain, do you understand, I am certain that he would be the first to refuse to have his name there, on the monument."

"That wouldn't surprise me," I say.

We had taken a few steps in the rain. The old woman in her

madras scarf was droning as always: "Buy my pretty carnations, buy my pretty carnations."

Bourladou bought flowers for Madame Bourladou.

"I'm adding some mimosa for you," the woman says. "Pure velvet, but they're like pretty women, they don't last."

As he was leaving me, Bourladou did not fail to ask after my book. It was going pretty well, thanks.

"I have been thinking just now about a title . . . "

"No kidding!" Bourladou exclaimed joyfully.

"*The Cattle Car*," I said. "Don't you think that would make a good title: *The Cattle Car?*"

Bourladou contemplated the flowers he was holding in his hand as though he expected enlightenment from them. Somewhere, within the framework of his two hundred and ten pounds, a mental phenomenon was in course, and it would turn out to be perplexity.

"It's a sort of symbol, you understand."

"Ah yes, right, a symbol."

Around us, in the provincial night, the place du Théâtre was empty, woebegone, and glistening with rain. An unpropitious place and time for symbols.

"Tell you what, you'll explain it to us one of these days," Bourladou hastily concluded.

He gave me a gracious little good-bye wave with the bouquet wrapped up in pretty paper.

Explain what? I was thinking of Marécasse in his striped rags. Marécasse whom they tossed in along with some others, as Bourladou puts it. Along with some others, at one end of a cattle car. He did not know why. Did the others know more than he? Even those who thought they knew? You submit uncomprehendingly, you scream justifications in the face of people who are deaf, as had the big German floundering about in front

of the snout of a machine gun. And in the end you resign yourself and shut up. I thought of my landlady. Of the Crabs. Of the
masses. Of all those people buried inside the mass of people,
locked up within events and things. I thought of Craquelou,
Barche, of my buddies from 1940. Of the snow-covered plains.
Of the freight trains that used to flow like slow gray worms over
the dead face of Europe.

Ulysse engage une vache
Pour chanter à son lutrin.
Vache vache herbivache
O les jolis trains à vaches
O la jolie vache à train.

—MAURICE FOMBEURE

Impossible to lie down there on your back, in the cattle car. Too many of us. But, provided everyone lay on his side and all fitted themselves tightly against each other, you managed to accommodate everyone. My belly adhered to Vignoche's buttocks, my buttocks to Chouvin's belly. No wasted space. All our fatigues wedged, glued, lumped together. This permitted a sort of clanking, dislocated drowsiness. The train rolled along within its stubborn din. Noise of the wheels, noise of the wheels. In the end you identify with the noise of the wheels. Then it would stop without our knowing why, one hour, two hours, and we would listen to the sentries tramping up and down the length of the convoy, listen to their raucous shoutings. And then the train would start rolling again. Noise of the wheels. The same thing for nights on end, across this country with stove-in borders. We would ask, where are they taking us? But the noise of the wheels soon stilled curiosities. Maybe we are not going anywhere. We are there. That's the way it is. A freight train crawling through an enormous silent disaster. Into it they have packed men instead of goods. The doors of the cars are fastened shut, bolted, padlocked. Nothing like it to instill in you the feeling of an inevitable fate.

Fate without a capital *f.* Not the Fate of the old tragedies, with its visage of stone. Those of us crammed in here are entitled only to a bleary-eyed, shoddy, broken-down fate. In the cattle car.

Halfway through the night, when our fatigue became intolerable, we would all of us together turn onto our other side; we would recreate in reverse our pattern of tightly overlapping bodies: my buttocks against Vignoche's stomach, Chouvin's buttocks against my stomach. This was the moment to take advantage of if you wished to piss into the tin can being passed from hand to hand. Watch out, someone would shout in the darkness, look where you're pissing, you asshole, it's landing on me. Afterward, we had to empty the receptacle out the car's ventilation window; Ure attended to that. The window was high up, narrow, and grilled by barbed wire. Ure almost always bungled the job.

These things belong to the most widely shared experience. We were millions who, for one reason or for another, had ourselves trundled around in freight cars. It's instructive: you get a precise idea of yourself. I am an object that weighs about one hundred twenty pounds and measures five feet seven. A parcel, but a thinking parcel, to paraphrase that other fellow. A conscious parcel, docile, that conforms ingeniously to its parcel's condition. It spontaneously takes its assigned place. It endeavors not to get in the way. You don't obtain that much from crates of soap or sacks of beans.

As dawn approached we would disentangle ourselves, undo the jumble of arms and legs. We would get part way up. We would lean against the wall. We would try all the different ways of evening out the stiffness and aches in one's body. To hurt, there's no avoiding that; but you can always hurt otherwise, transfer the aching from the shoulders to the knees, from the knees to the thighs. A body is full of resources if you know how to manage.

Sometimes we tried to see something through the wire-covered window. Nothing to see. Empty plains, a burned-out railway station. The war, Germany—maybe all that was over with. Perhaps the only thing left alive was this train hauling its lice-ridden freight toward no one knows what. We crossed a river: Chouvin thought it was the Elbe, another claimed it was the Weser. They got into a dispute. How about the Marne for a change, one guy asked. We laughed weakly. The guy's face had a bitter and crafty look, but it was his grime and hunger that gave him that expression. An average sort of guy, no doubt; not particularly smart; my kind. "It's because I'm from Epernay," he explained to me. His head and shoulders were shaking from the joltings of the train. All our heads, all our shoulders rattled up and down in unison. The guy added that he owned a bookstore.

"I do stationery, too, needless to say, and even fountain pen repairs."

He held a snapshot out to me, I don't know why. A picture of his wife; what the hell did I care about his wife? I gave it a look even so: the lady had heavy legs, jewels, jowls. She was closing her eyes because of the sunlight. I passed the picture to my buddies, who examined it one after the other. Ure said: "Goddamn."

"Things were going good," the Epernay guy was saying. "We were even thinking about buying ourselves a little place in the country . . . "

I had trouble hearing. Chatting wasn't easy, with that racket of the wheels filling your head. I shouted: "Buying what?"

"A little place," the Epernay guy shouted. "In the country. Except, well, the war came along . . . "

"What came along?" I shouted.

"The war," the Epernay guy shouted. "The war came along."

He smiled vaguely from the depths of his grime. You saw he was a man who submitted to what comes along. There's nothing you can do about it, it is there. Got to take what comes your way. Maybe he found it all astonishing, that these fluke occurrences should bust into the middle of an Epernay shopkeeper's life story. But thoughts and opinions were being swallowed up by the noise of the wheels. No point trying to outshout them. We live in peculiar times, that's all there is to it. The guy cautiously exercised his joints. There, that feels better. It was already over with, his attempt at a personal existence. After that he did not stir, reincorporated into the mass of undifferentiated rattling inside the cattle car. Noise of wheels. Noise of wheels. Peculiar times; but you adapt to peculiar times. You manage. The guy from Epernay had that profound, informed countenance you see on imbeciles and on the dead. The times—you get used to them. You settle into, you melt into onflowing events. Within them you let yourself be shaken, jolted, and tossed about as though you were inside a cattle car.

The word has finally gotten out that we have lost our bearings within the real. There are noble and abstract equivalents of cattle cars—history, morality, physics, politics. In times like these you find out depressing things about the cosmic and metaphysical position of man. But these speculations are above my comprehension. I am wary of excessive ambitions: in my moments of meditation (let's call them that) I confine myself to the trivial aspect of the cattle-car question. That is, to the experience of the absurd endured on the level of daily misery by the most ordinary individuals. Within these bounds I must say that I have acquired a certain competence. As a user of the cattle car, I belong to the current model. There can be no error here. I need but look at my reflection in the windows of the shops as I walk down the rue Douillet. It's mine, that gangling shape. It is that of a fifteen thousand-franc-a-month clerk, you can tell. That hangdog look, that tired outfit, they're me. A passerby, nondescript, looking vaguely run to earth. We are millions of identical passersby, millions upon millions of mirrored reflections. I, for one, know a fair number. Marécasse, or Dardillot, or my landlady, or my buddies from Company Five—nothing but people entangled like blindmen in the folds of a shapeless calamity. That will do by way of documentation. I would certainly have enough to compose a treatise on the cattle car. I shall have to give it some thought. It is, admittedly, a worn-out subject. Moreover, it leads straight to a drab naturalism, to that sort of adhesive and simplistic bitterness which noble souls so dislike. Madame Bourladou now: that would turn her stomach. She wants optimism and energy. A literature, as she often says, that has a feeling of grandeur. Unfortunately, the feeling of grandeur has not been granted to everyone. There are ill-favored natures that never behold things as they should be. I greatly fear that mine may be among those natures. It would perhaps require simply that I had Flouche's sonorous voice, or the powerful shoulders of Chancerel, the president of the Erection Committee, in order that I see the world in fine epic colors. It must be awfully satisfying to see it in red and gold, like a uniform from the days of the Empire. Instead of in these scabby browns, these pimply grays, these watery blacks of cattle-car flooring. But there's no help for it. It's a kind of infirmity I have, it affects my view. Grand words, grand attitudes arouse mistrust in me. I peer to the left or right, look for what's behind. I suspect parody, fakery, imposture, prefabricated enthusiasm, or self-delusion. I persuade myself that grandeur must be something utterly different—not oratorical, not official, not spectacular. That's what has prevented me, in particular, from finding in the global conflicts of the twentieth century those invigorating raptures that a war always procures for better-formed witnesses. If ever I compose my treatise on the cattle cars, I dare say it is there that I would have to begin—with a few little episodes from the international upheavals, which led me to think a bit, at certain moments in my life.

Before the warlike ceremony, walk away. If you have to remain, think about the dead, count the dead. Think about those blinded in the war, that cools one's passions. And for those who are in mourning, instead of becoming drunk and dazed upon glory, have the courage to be unhappy.

—ALAIN

My first contact with heroism dates from the other war, the Great One . . .

I was in middle school. Our teachers in French class dictated to us the best pages of Maurice Barrès, in order to train us in spelling and national spirit at one go.

The principal's son was killed in the Argonne. On that occasion his colonel addressed to the father a letter written in a very noble tone, in which he included (as one cultivated man speaking to another) a quotation in Latin. From Seneca, I believe. The principal insisted on reading and then discussing the letter before the pupils assembled expressly to that end. He was a giant of a man, with a purplish countenance, a brow one inch high, and Nietzsche's mustache.

A few years before that, another of his children had committed suicide. The maid had found him in the morning, curled up on the stone floor of the kitchen between a bottle of rum and an old revolver. Among the Families there was deep sympathy for the father. A man with a sense of duty. A man, the Families said, who didn't deserve such a thing, who had nothing to blame himself for. As for the dead boy, he had been nothing but a sickly and solitary figure when alive, unable to pass his exams.

The second loss made up in a way for the first. This time

things had a classic and official air. Suicide has within it something baffling, something suspect and rather sordid. It is one of those circumstances that put fathers of families in an uncomfortable position. But death on the field of honor is in agreement all at once with our ethical ideas, social conventions, and good literature. You have no trouble steering your way amid preestablished feelings and approved attitudes. The principal was perfect.

His spontaneously funereal aspect predisposed him to majestic sorrows. Nothing was wanting: neither the burning gaze, nor the gruff pride of the mustache, nor the stiffening of the torso, which denotes courageous acceptance. To read us the colonel's letter, he adopted the heavy, painstaking voice he used during the solemn awarding of class prizes. Upon reaching the sentence out of Seneca, he translated it for the pupils doing modern languages, then reread it in Latin, and, humanist that he was, a fleeting satisfaction mingled discreetly with his suffering as a father.

After his reading, in sober terms he recalled the figure of this son, who, he told us, had graduated high in his class from the National School of Engineering. It was a victim adorned with the most flattering university diplomas that he was offering to the fatherland. A hard sacrifice undoubtedly, but whose bitterness was attenuated by the colonel's letter. He had given his son to the fatherland, but he had the letter. It was an equitable exchange, their accounts balanced out. And by way of ending, the principal wished that this scene might engrave itself in our memories and inspire strong resolutions within us.

What it contained of the highly educational could have been compromised shortly afterward by the surprising conduct of our mathematics teacher. When he heard that his brother had likewise been gloriously killed, this professor, far from imitating the principal's stoic firmness, surrendered himself to rank despair.

We saw him rushing across the younger pupils' courtyard in the very middle of the ten o'clock recess. He was howling. A few colleagues got him bracketed, and the principal himself was coming up, gesticulating and breathless. The professor was struggling in their midst, and howling. True howls—not moans or cries. It was much more rudimentary, more primitive, more naked. Howling as in torture chambers and madhouses. It came from his entire body, it spouted out of him like blood, the school was awash in it, it filled the whole town. The kids witnessed this with the feeling that they had come upon an adults' secret, that they were seeing something they should not be seeing.

And indeed this spectacle was rapidly screened from us. It threatened to tear some necessary myths to pieces. Silence descended upon a deplorable incident. When the mathematics teacher reappeared, he had his ordinary appearance. It was that of a puny and timorous creature. In town people wondered sourly that he was not called up, although of age to bear arms. In reality, he was tubercular enough to put off the draft board each time it looked at his case, even though, at the time, they were not hard to please in their appreciation of human material.

The war ended a little later, and a memorial was erected to the dead.

It's since the monument to the dead that I know I sing off-key. No one had noticed it, because I never sing. Or if I do, it's only when I'm alone. But there was this monument to the dead to inaugurate. Everybody was given his role. The town councilmen, the policemen. The learned societies. The sons of the dead, the wives of the dead, the mothers and fathers of the dead. The only ones who had no role were the dead themselves, as their name implies. The role of the middle-school children was to sing "Those Who Piously Gave Their Lives for Their Country," words by Victor Hugo, music by Hérold. We had rehearsed it for one solid month. I can still see our teacher: an alcoholic old man with bloodshot eyes, a wet mustache, and thick veins on his hands. He would become riled. "That's not it, that's not it at all. Louder, for heaven's sake, now take it once again." We would make a still worse mess of it. "Stop, stop, that's a C-sharp," the drunkard would shout. And it was he who at once noticed that I was singing off-key! And that the whole choir was singing out of tune because of me, and that I was going to spoil the pious ceremony.

"Get the hell behind the others, and let's not hear another sound from you."

His reddened eyes blazed with scorn. I went and took a place at the back of the class. We were a half-dozen ninth-grade pupils subjected together to the same humiliation. Excluded from the music of Hérold and the words of Victor Hugo.

My mother brushed and shined me anyway, on Monument Day, and put a new tie on me. And I stood to the rear of those who could sing on key. Without a role to play. All I could do was watch the flags, the green plants, and the official jackets on which the rain was falling. Look at those who could sing on key singing. Look at the monument. It was a sort of wall, with, in gold letters, the Names arranged in columns in alphabetical order. A stone soldier, equipped with full battle gear, mask, rifle, helmet, and mustache, with one extended arm pointed out to a naked child (also in stone) a metal urinal, which stood modestly at the corner of the boulevard Désiré Lemesle and the rue des Deux-Eglises.

A vigorous allegory, which the most simpleminded of our compatriots would have been able to decipher. But our compatriots had other concerns. Each of them had himself become allegorical. Each widow was the Widow. Each former combatant, the Hero. Not one oldster who did not seem to have stepped out of the complete works of Corneille. And at the same time as the top hat, the veils of mourning, the reserve officer's decorations or uniform, they had all donned this particular nuance of resolution, of sadness, or of dignity that the circumstances demanded.

Far too taken up with their own roles to think about the dead. Anyway, to think about the dead was superfluous: henceforth that was what the monument was there to do. That was the monument's role. Stone wouldn't forget. The names were there, fixed, engraved, gilded; it was all done right. In a human being's memory, a remembrance is always fragile and insecure. In stone it stays put. On this day of rain and music, the twenty-three thousand inhabitants of my hometown solemnly discharged their obligation to maintain intact the image of Beaulavoir Alfred, who had been killed at Eparges, of Choupar Anatole, who had been killed near Albert. Thus assuring themselves the inward tranquillity necessary for digestion, copulation, card games, for the various kinds of human commerce. Nothing would be possible with the weight of the dead upon your thoughts. It was important to free the town from this pressure. To exorcise the collective conscience and the individual conscience of these tragic presences. The dead themselves gained therefrom. The dead ceased to be corpses, instead they became Names. They exchanged their wretched substance for a decorative abstraction. The algebraic elegance of letters inscribed in stone substituted itself for bloated and suppurating flesh, blinded eyes, torn-open bellies. Names were neat, they were clean. And even pretty to look at. And inoffensive, like a page from the dictionary or the telephone directory. Corpses are always full of reproaches and contempt. But, changed into names, they acquire a prodigious discretion. You read them without it occurring to you that they are the names of someone. You are not even compelled to read them.

My Uncle Aurélien, while at home on leave, had told us that one of his buddies had been buried by a shell: all that emerged was his foot, in its big hobnailed boot. They had left him like that. It was convenient, that foot. It served as a coat hook. You hung your cape there, your haversack. My uncle gave these details with satisfaction. "It's ghastly," my mother protested. "Come, come," my uncle answered with a laugh, "that's the way war is." At present, my Uncle Aurélien's utilitarian stiff has surely recovered its dignity, its decency. It must also have had its name inscribed on some monument. It was no longer a grotesque and incongruous object. It had attained the disincarnate universe of Names. It had taken on the nobility, the purity, the transcendence of Names. And if the image of that foot jutting out of the mud recurred to me again precisely at the moment the schoolchildren were singing "Those Who Piously Gave Their Lives for Their Country," the reason is that, when you are not in the choir, ideas come to you that you shouldn't have.

Those who sang on key were singing, and did not ask for anything more. Mouths opened and closed. The old alcoholic's hands rose and fell. One, two, three, four. Mouths, all together, became circular, became oval-shaped. The drunkard's lean hands drew their mechanical geometry in the air, one, two, three, four. Then they abruptly shot upward, and all the voices took wing. Then the hands mimicked a little fluttering of fins. And all the voices thinned. With his trembling blue hands the old drunkard stretched out, made swell, kneaded a sticky dough of voices.

Those who sang on key bathed in the great happiness of all sharing one voice. They were intoxicated with unanimity. That was to be seen in their bearing, self-important and tensed. In all those larynxes the same work was being performed at the same moment. The same irreproachable C-sharp was preparing itself in the same way down in all those throats. Heady satisfactions of similitude that were denied to me. Satisfactions I wasn't even able to conceive of. To me they looked idiotic, those who sang on key. When you look at others instead of being with others, you always think they look idiotic. All those mouths gaping the same way. And that seriousness, that application. They were certainly scared enough of missing that C-sharp of theirs.

Mouths formed into little hearts, little souls in chorus. The chorus sings away. It does not even know what it is singing. It knows nothing other than that it is singing. Glory to our immortal France. Words by Victor Hugo. Another one who used to sing on key, that Victor Hugo. With everybody, like everybody. For a century he had sung with his century, unflinchingly, at the top of his voice and with all his heart, and he had lots of heart and quite a voice. He had plenty of chest. Glory to our eternal France. Glory to those who died for her. A November drizzle was falling on the weeds of mourning, on the stone soldier, on Hérold's music. It had been necessary to open umbrellas. The professor's hands loosed shapes into the void. One, two, three, four. To the martyrs, to the brave, to the strong. To Beaulavoir Alfred. To Choupar Anatole. Rain was falling on the names. The voices gave forth fiercely. In time, identical, never too high, never too low. Nothing stood amiss. The minister, deep in his armchair, amid the flags and the green plants, was perhaps vaguely considering how easily men could be governed if they always sang this way, all in chorus. If one could just line them all up in a row and have them all singing in chorus. Marching in chorus, singing in rows. Just get them going. One, two, three, four. "To those their example inflames," the children were singing. All alike, each impeccable. Not an idea, not a worry, not a question. "And who will die," the children sang, with ecstatic energy. "And who will die, and who will die." The stone soldier was indicating the rue des Deux-Eglises urinal to the naked child, but it was clear that this edifice constituted only a provisional objective. "And who will die as they died," the children sang. The way the guy my uncle talked about died. The guy was busy eating some bread and sardines. He was thinking about the letters he had received. His wife was advising him that one of their cows was sick. A woman who lived next door was telling him that his wife was sleeping with the German prisoner. The guy chewed his sardines. What a bitch, he was thinking, within that ambiguous observation assembling some complex bitternesses. Thereupon the shell had put an end to his reflections, and the guy thereafter showed himself to the eyes of the living only in the form of that foot emerging from the mud like a foot from a bed too short for a sleeper too long. Who will die the way that guy died. Or otherwise. The ways of dying in a war come in an infinite variety, war has that in its favor. And afterward, you have your name on a monument. A minister comes from Paris just for that purpose. Little boys sing in chorus. The rain was falling on the new stone. The rain was falling gently on the minister's dreams.

He was not an important minister. The minister of the Postal and Telegraph Service maybe, or the Merchant Marine. For a little city like ours, and for our two hundred seventy-three local dead, one could not hope for a celebrated statesman. But the speech he delivered, and which I had trouble hearing, was appreciated by those who are up on speeches. My father praised it that evening, between the salad and the cheese. To be sure, all it took for my father to think a man was eloquent was for him to be a minister. My father firmly believed in the eloquence of ministers, as he did in the bravery of generals and the wisdom of professors.

The minister was thickset and stood rocking on short legs. Having finished his speech, he advanced toward the monument, step by step, heavily and clumsily. He resembled a large sluggish beast, awkward and enigmatic. With a gaze in which nothing could be read, he contemplated the white-gloved policemen, the black-veiled widows, the lined-up children, and the crowd beneath the rain. Swaying, massive, and solemn. A sort of sacred animal. He took another few heavy steps. Behind him advanced morning coats and uniforms. The audience remained avidly on the lookout for the manifestations of this minimal activity. As at the zoo it does those of the seals or the hippopotamus. In silence it considered the minister's swollen countenance, in the back of which, deep within a majestic torpor, some inconceivable meditation was going forward. The crowd was wondering what was going to happen next. Therewith one saw the minister advance another few steps, then halt in front of the stone soldier. The morning coats and the kepis halted behind him. Next, the minister indolently wobbled his cheeks and chins. His shoulders bent, his head bowed. And thus the minister remained. People jostled each other for a better view. Everyone was conscious that they had reached the great moment of the ceremony: the minister was communing with himself.

He communed with himself admirably. Without altering so much as one fold in the cloth so nobly draped over his ministerial buttocks. Since then I have observed several ministers performing the exercise of self-communion: none appeared to me to attain the degree of perfection of that one. That self-communion contained such a quality of silence and stillness that it seemed that the minister had backed still farther into the realm of absence, of mindlessness and of opaqueness. He had reached a petrified grandeur, a geological dignity. The onlookers marveled that it was carried off so successfully and for so long. For one minute at least. For one whole minute the minister was this unhearing, unmoving, mineral block, this dark aerolith dug into the ground in front of the Names. Then, very simply, he ceased being rock, he reintegrated himself into the animal kingdom. He shook himself. He moved off. His escort moved off likewise. On his stubby legs the minister, step by step, headed toward the families of the dead and the delegations of war veterans. While passing in front of us, he shook the hand of our music teacher. Though I was in the last row, I could see from fairly near on his vast, desertlike face in which his short mustache looked pink.

Into the breach yet again? As often
as you wish, General.

—PAUL CLAUDEL

Since then, the stone soldier has aged considerably. I was looking at him this evening while crossing the place du Président-Doumerche. He has lost his jauntiness and his confidence. The rain and sun have given him a pitted, mournful, distraught countenance. I found him rather to my liking. He is beginning to resemble my Company Five comrades, my mates in the huts and the cattle car.

If in keeping with the old artifices of classical rhetoric I were to give him the power of speech, I know just what kind of things he would be apt to say. More or less the same things the guys around me would come out with in that village in the north of France where we had been brought together by the 1939 mobilization. A village that lay enveloped by nettles, seas of liquid manure, and the odor of cattle. Nothing was happening in that neck of the woods. History was still showing consideration, it hadn't begun its assault upon us. It enjoys roundabout ways and hitting below the belt. But we were suspicious. This won't last, the guys in my company were saying as with a knowing look they peeled the skin from their sausage during the midday break for lunch. It would be too good to be true, just imagine.

However, they would have been pleased as can be had it lasted. They were in no hurry to receive their ration of historic catastrophe. They were fellows who got no special kick out of soldiering, and who weren't particularly eager to risk their skin. Theirs was not particularly youthful skin, moreover. It had already seen thirty or forty years of service. For thirty or forty years it had dried up, gotten scraped, been creased, become scarred. But worn and down at the heels though it was, they were attached to it.

They peered with hostility at the dull Flemish plain under its sooty and rainy sky. Peasant women in rubber boots were pulling up beets. Bent low to the ground, they moved forward, cut off the leaves, tossed the root to one side. Two-phase work: cut, toss, cut, toss. The same thing all day long. Lousy work, the guys would say.

They would describe their own work to one another, their lives. Lousy work also, and lousy lives. And at present here they were without even knowing why, hanging around like a bunch of jerks. They talked about the Polish woman who sold wine for five francs a liter. You need at least three to feel a little drunk. What a bitch, the guys would say. But several appreciated her sprinter's thighs and her lewdly suggestive expressions.

The redhead on the place de l'Eglise was also coveted by some. A puny little whore, probably diseased.

"Not even with a ten-foot pole," Pignochet would say.

"You're too picky," Manesse would say.

"Not even with the end of my cane," Pignochet would say.

"It's ass, isn't it?" Manesse would insist.

The chorus would approve: yes, it was ass, it definitely was.

"And if you want my opinion," Manesse would say, "a man, what I call a man, when he's got the urge he doesn't hem and haw, one way or the other he's got to get it off, that's the way it is."

Talk which, obviously, was not commensurate with events. Company Five lacked freshness of spirit, breadth of outlook, and any aptitude for general ideas. Here, thinking never ventured beyond the detail and the immediate. Bedding and the daily rations.

"We have a right to three packs of shag," Ravenel declared in the center of a vehement circle.

Barche, beheld to be an anarchist and a big talker, spat out his cigarette stub with authority. "Your rights now add up to zero. Get that into your head, kiddo. Zero. Got it? The only right you have left is to keep your trap shut."

"That may well be," Ravenel answered. "Still, as far as tobacco goes, we have a right to three packs, it's in the newspaper." He didn't know that he also had a right to a fragment of that shell from a seventy-five which, exploding a little short, put an end, six months later, to the demands of Private Ravenel, while he was doing K.P. duty.

I was pretty soon deprived of the benefit of these controversies. One morning, Captain Lebiche had me called in. "So then," he asked me, "you're the bachelor of letters?" I answered that I was. Company Five boasted hairdressers and waiters, a crooner, a pimp, a dozen vague sort of shopkeepers, and a good number of country boys. But I was the only one with a bachelor's degree. The captain went: "Fine, fine." He had the face of a sheep, narrow and perplexed. All the while bleating his "Fine, fine," he directed his ovine stare at my badges and the folds of my greatcoat. He seemed to be looking for something there, proofs of my culture perhaps. In the end, having judged, weighed, sized me up, and gotten a good grasp of me, Captain Lebiche decided that he would use me in the company office.

I was back to keeping records. History assigned me an unglamorous role in the Second World War. That did not displease me. Might as well write things down as unload trucks full of sand with my buddies. I am not all that fond of the outdoors and manual jobs. We were all right in the Company Five office: a big room that smelled of saltpeter and cat piss. On the mantle was a bronze elephant whose trunk served as a stand for a barometer. Captain Lebiche frequently studied this object with humorless wonder.

I am back with bottles of red ink, files, documents in longhand. It is just about the same as at Busson Brothers. I reproduce account statements in triplicate. Next to me, Douve is deep into a count of shovels, pickaxes, and wire cutters. He looks disgusted. Not because of the pickaxes; it's just a look that he has. It comes from his lips being turned down at the corners. Douve, in civilian life, is a Christian Brother. The staff sergeant sometimes tries to get a theological discussion going with him:

"And what about the Trinity, how do you explain that stuff, the Trinity?"

The little brother shrugs. Not at all a bad fellow, he is by nature somewhat lethargic. He has no desire to evangelize sergeants. "As you like," the staff sergeant says, miffed. And, to avenge himself, he proposes to tell us the story of his aunt from Bolbec.

"Perhaps I've already told it to you?"

"Not at all," Malebranche and I promptly assert.

"Well then, here goes," the staff sergeant says. "When my aunt from Bolbec died . . . "

When his aunt from Bolbec died and was laid to rest, the staff sergeant's family gathered for one of those ritual meals that distract the survivors from unduly depressing thoughts.

"I see," Malebranche says, "it hadn't got to you up until then."

"It wasn't so bad," the sergeant admits.

When they were about to bring the coffee on, they had, in accordance with custom, placed a bottle of Calvados on the table. It was spelled out on the bottle: Calvados. With the producer's name, the date, everything. So they proceeded to fill the glasses. All well and good. They clinked glasses. They drank their aunt's Calvados. They exchanged glances, nobody breathed a word. They clinked glasses again, drained them again. But about then one of the cousins decided to speak up. "Don't you think," the cousin asked, "that the old lady's Calvados tastes funny?" Of course, everybody thought that it had tasted funny. Better still, it hadn't had any taste at all. They had pretended not to notice anything, out of politeness. But they entirely agreed: for Calvados, it lacked kick. "You might even say it tastes more like water," the cousin went on. And do you know what their aunt's Calvados actually was?

"How could we?" Malebranche says.

"It was holy water," the staff sergeant says.

"Well, how about that!" Malebranche says.

"Holy water," the staff sergeant says. "Just wait till you hear how that happened."

He explains that the women in the neighborhood had searched their aunt's house from top to bottom but in it there was not one drop of holy water to be found. Their aunt was not the kind of woman who went in for all that. They had had to run over to the presbytery. That's how it had happened.

"They'd just grabbed the first bottle they saw, you understand. None other than that damned bottle of Calvados that was sitting right there . . . "

The three of us laugh very loudly. Douve, with his expression of permanent disgust, bends over his sums. He's not good at addition. He always ends up with too many pickaxes or too few wire cutters. Which provokes Captain Lebiche's rancorous wonder: "A lad like you, with your education—frankly, it's beyond me . . . "

Reserve Captain Lebiche was short on imagination. Earlier confined within some subaltern employment at the Banque Nationale de Crédit, the importance he owed to the war at once intoxicated and overwhelmed him. Seated at his table, he respectfully handled the typewritten sheets that lay before him, followed the text word for word, and his little gray eyes would betray the efforts at concentration of an overtaxed intelligence.

When not sure he had grasped whatever it was, he would call upon the staff sergeant: "Tell me, how do you interpret this memorandum?"

It's the memorandum that has to do with rations of forage. Or else the memorandum on unexploded grenades. Or the memorandum on the destruction of hedges and fences. Or the memorandum on the correspondence with the graduates of the University of Pennsylvania.

"Let's see now," the staff sergeant says.

He in his turn enters into a brown study. Then, cautiously, he ventures an opinion, and the captain meditates upon the opinion he has just heard the staff sergeant venture.

If he finds himself troubled by problems of expression, he turns instead to Malebranche, who from his bourgeois origins preserves a nice sense of the proper phrase. Malebranche's father was a subprefect. He himself is not anything precise. He claims that he published medical works at a certain moment in his life. He would also have spent a little time selling cars.

"Tell me, Malebranche," says the captain, who for the past twenty minutes has been fine-tuning the grounds for a penalization, "tell me, in your opinion would it be better to write 'while drunk, struck a comrade' or 'while in a state of inebriation'?"

Malebranche pretends to weigh the pros and cons.

"Basically, sir, basically it comes down to the same thing."

"Yes," the captain says, "but 'while in a state of inebriation' sounds better, don't you think? 'While in a state of inebriation . . .'"

This one, this state of inebriation, is not rare among the men of Company Five. On this particular occasion, Barche, drunk as a skunk, got into a fight with Ravenel. The victim had come in to offer for Captain Lebiche's pity a swollen face decorated with little crosses of adhesive tape. The captain questioned Barche.

"We had a controversy," Barche explains.

"You were drunk," the captain says.

"I'd had a drink," Barche concedes.

"And you struck your comrade?"

"Some blows were exchanged," Barche admits.

Thereupon, the captain, mindful of his men's moral behavior, undertakes to dictate to Malebranche a memorandum that will be read out to the assembled company standing at attention:

"Drunkenness turns a man into an animal who acts often comma if not always comma like a fool period. The company commander calls upon the good sense of each man comma in order that a brake be placed upon alcoholic beverages period."

The final metaphor induces a ripple of muffled hilarity among the scribes. Once the captain is out of the office, the epithets come forth: "The stupid bastard," "A pain in the ass." Servile performances. Malebranche, who possesses, as his one apparent gift, a curious talent for imitating, installs himself before the typewritten directives.

"Let's see now, how would you interpret this memorandum?"

Captain Lebiche's voice to perfection—that combination of authority and uneasiness. You'd have sworn it was the captain speaking.

"Do the bugle thing," the staff sergeant pleads.

"Oh yes," Douve says, "do the bugle for us."

The bugle scene fetches something close to a laugh from even the cheerless Douve.

Several days ago, the division had asked for men who were able to blow a bugle. Private Marceau had presented himself at the company office, and the captain submitted him to a close examination.

"Ah, so you're Private Marceau?"

Malebranche becomes Private Marceau. Simpleminded, mouth agape, stammering speech, cap between his fingers: "Marceau, yes, Captain. Marceau, Ildefonse, Captain. Number 72887, Captain."

Now Malebranche adopts, instantaneously, a mask of majestic imbecility. One recognizes Captain Lebiche's look. Absolutely on target: it's the face of a sheep. And Captain Lebiche's voice is heard: "So, you know how to blow a bugle? . . . Fine, fine.

We'll see how you do. Could you play . . . let's see, could you play 'To the General'?"

"Oh yes, Captain."

Malebranche has turned back into Private Marceau. Private Marceau stands at attention. He raises his chin. To his lips he brings a hand grasping an imaginary trumpet. And at the top of his lungs: "Tatata tatata, tatata tatata."

"Fine, very fine," Malebranche says, who has switched back to sounding and looking like Captain Lebiche. An impartial and scrupulous Lebiche. Bent on not allowing a doubtful *tatata* to get by. Imbued also with a subtle delight characteristic of the artist.

"Fine, fine. And now, let's see, how about 'To the Flag'? Think you're able to play 'To the Flag'?"

"Oh yes, Captain."

Heels together, feet at a right angle, chin upraised, Malebranche cuts loose: "Tatata tatata, tatata tatata."

"Fine, fine," he says afterward, nodding Captain Lebiche's head. "And 'To the Parade'? . . . Play 'To the Parade' for us . . . "

Thus did we spend our days. Germany had invaded Poland. The Russians were fighting in Finland. Douve was endlessly counting tools, handkerchiefs, undershorts, pairs of socks, colic belts, gas masks, mugs, and canteens. A disagreeable, sticky, yellowish winter overlay the plain where Company Five pursued its obscure destinies. There was a fifty-centime increase in the price of a liter of red wine. An attempt on Hitler's life failed. In Neufchâtel-en-Bray (Seine-Inférieure), the husband of Malebranche's sister-in-law found her in bed with a British sergeant. It was being said that some murky business was afoot out in Turkey or up in Norway. Aragon published love poems inspired by the circumstances. Estevel fell from a loft and broke his leg. He was in a state of inebriation, despite Captain Lebiche's memorandum. "And I'd warned them, too," the captain lamented. "It cannot be said that I am to blame."

It was all part and parcel of the same thing, all that. You didn't know how, but it was all connected. Necessary and mysterious relationships bound together these events of seemingly disparate size.

Snow was starting to fall. We received the order to move out. Company Five was bounced around for a few hours in a train of cattle cars and finally dumped on the edge of a village like the one it had left.

"Doesn't look like it's going to be any fun in this place," the disappointed guys were saying.

"It'll be just right for us," Barche rejoined bitterly. "Whether we're here or somewhere else."

"Yeah, well, still," the guys were saying, "it looks pretty grim."

We took up quarters in what people in the village called the Château. A somewhat removed structure, dilapidated and ramshackle now, but which in bygone days had sheltered privileged existences: there were suggestions of this in the elaborately wrought ceilings, the vastness of the rooms, and the traces of gilt persisting on the woodwork. All around extended a nobly laid-out garden in which clumps of box were rotting. The rusted grillwork, the ivy upon the walls, and the effects of the snow conferred upon this locale a poetic something altogether out of Verlaine. At the farther end of the garden, on Captain Lebiche's orders and in conformance with regulations, we dug a deep and narrow ditch over which a few planks were placed, so that the men of Company Five could there satisfy their needs.

It continues to snow. The war continues. Douve continues to do his sums and to do them improperly. For our keeping of accounts we had requisitioned a downstairs room in the house of the Widow Passegrain. The photograph of the late Passegrain adorns one of its walls: a comely gentleman without forehead or neck, presenting a massive mustache, not an easy customer from the look of him. Captain Lebiche, seated underneath the picture of the deceased, is choosing the terms of a report to the battalion commander:

"Let's see, Malebranche, do you say 'covinance' or 'connivance'?"

"You say 'connivance,' Captain."

"Oh, you do? With one *n*, correct?"

"With two, Captain."

Malebranche's humor, since the Neufchâtel-en-Bray scandal, has darkened. Letters from his wife are becoming rare, and he has forebodings. When the staff sergeant asks him to do the bugle scene, he sternly tells the staff sergeant to leave him alone.

"Okay," the staff sergeant says. "Sure."

And he leafs through moldy magazines, *Match*, *Voilà*, a collection of which we discovered in the Widow Passegrain's closets. They're educational. In them you can contemplate old ministers, old actresses. The staff sergeant formulates indecorous comments on the thighs of theater women, without shaking my comrade Douve from his chronic apathy. Douve is wandering in a desert of figures. The figures are now suddenly exuberant, now hypocritically uncompliant. Their own way, malicious and inflexible, of eluding Douve's enterprises. Douve knows that he'll never make his way out of it. Sometimes, reaching the bottom of a page, you think it's going to tally, but there's always something that doesn't tally. All you can do is start over. Douve is patient. He starts over, neither hoping nor despairing. Like that he is ready to spend eternity reconstructing his mathematical desert. He expects nothing from figures, nor from anything else. Nothing from nothing. He has made his the great wisdom of the war.

Not far off, Company Five is putting up a series of plank

huts. It is not known why. That's all part of the war. The planks, the figures. In the evening, after supper, the guys flounder through the village snow. They have a drink, they have a screw, depending on the opportunities. Then they go off to sleep in their straw, in the Château. It's not warm in that big son of a bitch of a place. And there's Craquelou scratching himself all night—he contracted mange; they gave him shots, in the hospital, and they say it's cured; but he continues to scratch.

"You could maybe have caught the syph or something, huh?" asks Pignochet.

"The syph, will you listen to that," Craquelou protests, "the syph."

"He's going to give it to all of us," says Barche.

"But I've been telling you that it's cured," Craquelou whines. "They told me at the hospital, and you aren't going to tell me they don't know."

There you have it, their life. An aimless little life of fretting and peevishness. The impoverishment of men in the army. The sluggish, the ponderous, the ludicrous misery of men in the army. It's without interest. Soldiers, it's when they fight that they become interesting. Or when they go by in a street with bandages and crutches. You have to see how women look at them then. But these men here are not fighting. They're just barely good enough for putting up wooden shacks in some place off in the country that History seems to have forgotten about. They're not even young. And, oh my, what dash. No dignity, little discipline. And then their foul language, their jokes, their puerile rages: truly a bunch of clods. That's what Captain Lebiche was given to command. Clods. Animals.

"Come have a look at this—really, come have a look."

The captain had gone for a walk in the park of the Château. In the large, frozen, solitary park. He came back almost immediately, consternated by what he had discovered. Ah, the pigs.

You simply have to come look at this. We all go out, the staff sergeant in the lead. We enter the glittering domain, all pink spangles under the morning sky.

"Eh?" the captain says. "What do you think of that?"

"What do I think?" the staff sergeant says. "What do I think?"

What could he think? The situation is clear, explicit, broadly on display.

"Suppose," says the captain, "suppose the colonel had come upon this?"

A confused retrospective terror adds itself to the captain's indignation. Ah, the pigs. He paces furiously, cautiously, about the snow-covered grass. The pigs. The pigs. With a deerskin-gloved hand he points one by one to the scandal's various aspects: "Look, over there. Another there. And there. And there."

It's all over the place. The company does things in a broad style. Soiled pieces of paper—water-stained letters, fragments of the *Echo du Nord*—bestrew the aristocratic pathways. "Nice mess," the captain repeats. The four scribes, behind him, nod their heads with an expression usually reserved for great tragedies. With its native air of disgust, Douve's physiognomy is wonderfully in keeping with the situation.

"It defies the imagination," the captain moans.

Much good it did to have had the regulation-size pit dug and planks placed across the hole. When the guys get up at night, shivering all over, they judge the pit too far away, and the planks so slippery, with their accumulation of frozen snow, that the worst mishaps are to be feared. And so they hurry outside and squat down anywhere. They relieve themselves in haste, and run back and bury themselves in their straw under their cotton blankets. That's what is defying Captain Lebiche's imagination.

He makes some decisions. He is a man of decision, the captain. Order to Sergeant Tombedieu to assemble a six-man detail and to dispose of those indecent hillocks; and to see to it that no trace whatsoever remains of them; and to attend to this without one minute's delay.

"There's a job they can get their teeth into," the captain flings at Sergeant Tombedieu.

And henceforth rigorous sanctions are in store for whoever fails to use the official sheets of paper for his necessities.

At the office we laugh about the incident for the next two weeks. Only the late Passegrain does not appear to find it so funny. He goes on scowling at us from inside his black and gold frame. Eventually it gets on our nerves. Surely in agreement with Captain Lebiche, that citizen up there. On the side of order, of seriousness, of hygiene, and of legality. Malebranche, become tart what with his private worries, has developed an aversion for the deceased. He directs insults at him all day long.

"Son of a bitch. Old son of a bitch. Dirty old son of a bitch. Son of a son of a bitch."

He stares ferociously at that cantankerous mustache, at those dead eyes: "Good God, just look at that moronic face, will you."

A face like that face proclaims an orderly existence, exact, compact, unflinching. The face of the man who's got it right, who's never in the wrong, always on time, who's vaccinated, confessed, insured, not one paper missing, all his buttons buttoned. "A bitch. You're a real bitch, you are." One of those whose addition was always correct. And who stayed on the right. Always. And who never drove in the wrong direction on a one-way street. And who didn't eat meat on Fridays. Malebranche's animosity infects all of us. We cry forth to one another the innumerable virtues in Milord Passegrain's possession. It organizes itself into a kind of litany, into a rudimentary poem.

"He wasn't the sort of fellow," the staff sergeant says, "who would have shit on the boards."

"Or pissed against the doors," Malebranche says.

"Or spit in the subway," I say.

"Or smoked at the movies," the staff sergeant says.

And all together, caught up in a lyrical furor, confronting the inaccessible, the intangible, the everlasting Passegrain, we sing:

He never stepped
Outside his role,
He didn't shit
Beside the hole.

Even I, who, however, do not sing in tune. Even Douve.

"What's going on in there?" demands Captain Lebiche, bursting in upon us at the height of the uproar, with that dumbfounded-sheep look of his.

The staff sergeant stammers. We quickly return to our ledgers. Passegrain remains on top.

As always. It's always Passegrain who wins. Passegrain, Lebiche, those folks. We can dig each other in the ribs and exchange grins on the sly all day long, they'll still have the last word. They'll keep giving us the shaft until the end of time. This is only the beginning. They're the stronger ones. Because they never fool around, not they. About anything. For them there isn't any comic side to things. Or any grotesque side. The futile, the absurd, the sordid, none of that exists for them. Have a little patience: we're not done seeing what they're capable of. We'll see everything being administered. Poverty, fear, hunger. Everything being methodically organized. Decline. Despair. Everything being calculated, arranged, regulated, allowed for, planned. Flesh and blood, muscles, brain, intestines, bladders, shit and death. With, to keep the machine running, serious-minded people, imperturbable technicians, bureaucrats in reinforced concrete. The age belongs to them. We're going to see that. And instead of fooling around, it would be better if we did some thinking.

"And regarding that matter of the latrines, where do we stand at present?"

It is to Lieutenant Marole, his adjutant, the captain has put his question. Solemnly. In the tone one might use when consulting a specialist about the latest findings on pre-Columbian art.

Lieutenant Marole used to teach history in a lycée in Brittany. He has moved from theory to practice: he is overseeing the construction of the huts, even though nothing up until now would appear to have prepared him for this modest form of military activity. Each evening, on his return from the construction site, he sits down by the stove, smokes his pipe, and reads clauses five and six, which supplement administrative decision number forty-three. What he thinks about them is not known.

"Regarding the matter of the latrines," he declares evenly, "this is the shape it has taken."

He unfolds the shape the matter of the latrines has taken. A sober, precise exposé. And this splendid professorial voice, which never stumbles, which does not miss a syllable. Listening to it is a delight. You understand that it serves some purpose to have graduated from the Ecole Normale Supérieure.

The huts that Company Five is building are intended to house a battalion. A battalion, that's around a thousand men. Hence one must foresee toilets for a thousand men. Well now, what does a thousand men represent? The problem lies therein. What can a thousand men produce in three months? Lieutenant Marole has made his calculations. Every consideration taken into account, he estimates that one may anticipate ninety cubic meters of matter. One mixed into the other.

"That's not enormous," muses Lebiche.

"I am establishing these evaluations," Lieutenant Marole makes clear, "on the basis of one liter per day per man."

"That seems a little short to me," the staff sergeant remarks.

"Really?" the lieutenant says.

According to the staff sergeant, with two liters per man per day you would be within reality.

"As much as that," Lebiche exclaims in surprise.

"You are omitting an important element," rejoins the professor.

His accent betrays a hint of sly superiority, as though he were unmasking an aberrant proposition in a tenth grader's exercise. Douve is listening with interest to this debate on men and numbers.

"You are not taking into account a surely regrettable but nonetheless constant practice in the French Army," says the professor. "Namely, that of reserving latrines for the solider excretions and of urinating in the natural environment."

The captain sighs. "Moreover," Lieutenant Marole adds, "I am proceeding here from the most favorable hypothesis." The staff sergeant ponders the lieutenant's objection. It has weight to it. After having muttered "Of course" and "When all is said and done," he concedes that with one liter you ought to be able to do pretty well.

"You need have no doubt about it," says the professor.

He smokes his pipe. A studious silence settles over them. The late Passegrain's consequential presence reminds us that this is no laughing matter.

"I have given it a great deal of thought," the captain says the next day. "I have given a great deal of thought to this matter of the latrines. For my part I'd put it up there around a liter and a half."

We were at war. When rather than thinking about men they're thinking instead about cubic meters of human flesh or human waste, it's because war has come. Whether they call it by that name or by some other.

We were at war, but you could not really tell. The outward signs weren't there—the ruins, the corpses. That is still to come. We shall have them in the spring, corpses blooming in the fields, smashed corpses, wide open, offered to the sunny skies and to the rainy skies. For the moment, you have the impression that nothing is stirring. The village is asleep, lost within winter, with its fountain wrapped up in straw, with its naive grocery and general store where you can buy stationery and thermos bottles. We scribble away in our little corner, without seeing any farther than our record-keeping. Sometimes Malebranche takes out a snapshot of his wife, then sticks it back into his wallet. Captain Lebiche is absorbed in calculations for cesspits. One liter and a half per man per day, for a battalion, that comes to one hundred thirty-five cubic meters per trimester. Provided the men use the privies. That will have to be seen to. No tolerating certain personal predilections or unwarranted anarchical manners of handling oneself.

Barche explains to the slaves flopped about in their straw, "You don't even have the right to shit where you please."

"You didn't before either," Ravenel points out.

"It wasn't the same thing," Barche says. "Before the shit-houses, the idea of not using them would never even have entered your head. Had to be a slob for that. While now, slob or not a slob, you don't give a damn. And even, in a way, you'd just as soon be a slob. That shows that you know you don't count anymore. You try to count, but you don't count anymore."

With the point of his knife he scrapes the thick mud from his shoes.

"You don't count anymore. Everything's decided without you, you don't know where or how. You, you're nothing. You don't mean anything anymore. All you can do is go in the direction you're pushed. You have no choice. Go where you're pushed and button your lip."

Having failed to get this theory of troubled times through his head, one of the Company Five guys took off without leave and got picked up by the gendarmes. What aggravated our buddy's case was that he bore the same name as the captain. There was nothing he could do about that, obviously. To him it would have been all the same to be called, for instance, Lebouc or Leloup, Lelièvre or Leboeuf. But his name happened to be Lebiche. That's the way it was. An accident, but one to which circumstances gave a tendentious character and a provocative appearance.

"What the bloody hell! Incredible!" the captain stormed as he walked around the table where the pen pushers were pushing their pens.

In itself, Private Second Class Lebiche's behavior lay within the everyday and predictable forms of military misconduct. But added to it was this homonymy, insidiously damaging to the hierarchical principle and constituting, in the captain's eyes, an elusive insolence and an ill-defined offense.

"Get this gentleman in here," he ordered.

Private Second Class Lebiche appeared. A long, gray-colored fellow with a gaunt face. He had the second-class smell— of straw, of damp, of leather, and of gun grease. The captain sniffed his homonym with distaste. The homonym saluted, took off his forage cap, waited. Faded red hair curled over violet ears. He had a somewhat shady look, unwashed, not very harmful.

The captain opened with some virtuous language, talk about one's native land, duty, court-martial. The fellow stood there without moving. His stiff, angular greatcoat looked as though it were cut from khaki-colored cardboard. Monstrous hands hung from its sleeves. With hands like those, it wouldn't be difficult to strangle a captain.

"You've put me in a pretty situation," the captain was saying in a sour voice.

Private Lebiche was thinking that you had to call this awful luck. The company was full of guys who had gone quietly over the fence for a couple of days without that causing any uproar.

And then there was him, stupidly going out for a fuck. Stupid, that was the word for him.

"Did you give even one moment's thought to your duty as a soldier?" the captain was asking.

When it's between you and a buddy, that's all right; you can explain. But with guys like this one here, you don't know how to go about it. They bring out these big words of theirs. Duty. You are at a loss for what to answer them. On the wall, Monsieur Passegrain's portrait shone with an austere vividness. Duty. Duty had a big mustache and well-fed cheeks. Duty was an enormous cop, smooth and calm, who would spot you from a distance, and sidle up nice as could be, and then light on you, and that does it, he's got me. Awful luck.

Soldier Lebiche did finally venture, feebly: "I needed to see my wife. That was the reason. I absolutely had to see her."

He found nothing else to oppose to the captain's stirring abstractions—his wife. What more did the captain want? My wife, Leona. He had talked to the gendarmes about his wife. They had said that they had orders. It's not that we're particularly mean bastards, the gendarmes had said. But we've got orders.

The captain was shrugging his shoulders: "Your wife?"

He, the captain, he, too, has a wife. A comfortable wife. An ample and flowery Madame Lebiche. She calls him my little bunny. She gives him cuff links for his birthday. And yet, what the bloody hell, he would not dream for one second of weighing his conjugal happiness against his soldier's duties.

"My wife," Private Lebiche said. "Well, I say my wife, though she isn't my wife. She isn't my wife though she is, seeing as how we live together."

"If I understand correctly," says Captain Lebiche, "you are not married."

"Oh yes, captain. Sure I'm married. I have a wife. The only thing is that the woman I'm with isn't my wife."

He brings forth his words very slowly, like heavy and dangerous objects. Words are treacherous. If you don't watch out, God knows where they'll land you. The best would be to keep still, but you haven't the right. I've already said too much for sure. That's what happens: talk, and you've gone too far. Yes, the captain is shaking his head. He is putting things in place. "Well, well," he is saying. You sense that he is coming upon some intriguing perspectives.

"Well, well now . . . So then, you live with a concubine?"

Private Lebiche answers neither yes nor no. For him there's Leona. Could be she's what the captain says. There's Leona who came with him to the station when they had the mobilization, the customers can wait for once, and she wanted to carry his haversack, come on, let me, you'll have plenty of time to lug it around, and she had a funny little trembly smile, and then she started to bawl, in the middle of the station, just nerves is what she said, she couldn't stop, it's stronger than I am, it's nerves.

"And so it was to rejoin a concubine that you deserted your post?"

The guilt of Private Second Class Lebiche is acquiring shape, taking on style, weight, and substance. He feels it slowly thicken. Nothing to be done: once you're jinxed, no point in struggling. His heavy hands dangle: they seem not to belong to him.

"A concubine," the captain repeats, "a concubine."

He is spellbound by the term. It smacks, he finds, of the official, the contemptuous, the distinguished. He eyes this fellow packaged in khaki cardboard. He sniffs his gray and greasy odor. Sentences of the report he'll draw up on this affair sketch themselves out and float inside his sheep's brain. "From the investigation I conducted, it results that this soldier has lived in concubinage ever since . . . "

"How long ago did you leave your legitimate wife?"

"I didn't leave her, she walked out on me," the fellow says.

"I'd have gone on being patient. She was the biggest whore you ever saw, but even so I'd have gone on. But she walked out on me."

He grows heated. His voice, his hands come back to life. A sudden eagerness gets into him. Because on this score at least he is comfortable in his mind. He's got proof. Here, wait a second. He rummages in his pockets. He paws through bits of paper, cards, newspaper clippings, snapshots. He becomes confused. Where the devil did I put that thing? His big hands panic. Like a pair of blind animals his hands climb up into his coat, poke about in folds, plunge, grope, bring to light and reject things. I just can't have lost it, that's all I'd need. No, here it is. He pushes a tattered letter toward the captain. Look. The captain is going to realize what sort of woman she was, that wife of his.

"What's that?" the captain asks.

"A letter," the fellow says.

"I can see that," the captain says.

"A letter from my wife," the fellow says. "My wife, Marthe, the one where we're married. She left me a letter when she dumped me. All you have to do is take a look at it. It's all there, in the letter."

"Very well, let's have a look then," the captain says.

"She'd left it on the sideboard," the fellow says.

The captain looks at the letter: a mean piece of paper, soiled, awful. He turns it over, then over once more. It has the smell of the poor, of the down and out. The fellow has reread it a good many times, has shown it to his friends. He uses it to bring back his sorrow and his anger. To preserve them intact. He needs them, both his sorrow and his anger. He's attached to them. They are part of him. It picks him up, puts new heart into him.

"She took everything, Captain, everything we had. The alarm clock, the hooch, the radio which wasn't even paid off yet. I see the letter on the sideboard. Well, Captain, I understood right away. I sure did. I was expecting it, in a way, seeing as we weren't getting on. But it hit me pretty hard even so."

The captain laboriously deciphers the document. Now and then he emits an "All right, all right," a "Well, well." Sometimes he stumbles over a poorly written word, and Private Lebiche leans forward in order to help him, rectifies an error, fills in a detail.

"This Denise . . . Who is this Denise person?"

"A friend," the fellow answers.

"And here? What's this here?"

"That's 'boor,'" the fellow says. "It's insulting me."

The captain raises his head. He taps his index finger upon a passage in the letter: "You wife claims that you used to beat her. Is that correct?"

"Of course," the soldier answers placidly.

"You used to beat your wife!" the captain cries indignantly.

(Phrases flutter about in his mind. "Subjected his legitimate wife to the worst brutalities . . . " It will be in the report. Spelled out clearly.)

"Had to," Private Lebiche explains. "A slut like her. Sometimes she'd stroll in at two in the morning. Sometimes she didn't come home at all. With bitches like that, you've got no choice."

To him it seems obvious, fair, proper. His acts are in agreement with the moral code of all poor devils. And he is ready to enter at length into the tale of his grievances and his grudges. But the captain's voice explodes: "A pretty business. Striking a woman. And you find that natural, do you?"

Private Lebiche is not insistent. Where would it get him to insist? The things you say to guys like this are always turned around against you. They don't have the same way of seeing things. Now the captain is singing his old song again. Family. Dignity. Back to his claptrap. All this over some no-good female who used to get herself fucked by anything in pants. And who'd scream at me, should have seen it. Hell yes, I'd swing at her, had to. What the hell does he care, the captain? It's just my business, after all. What's he going to ask next? Whether I've got kids? Yes, Captain, I've got one kid. And it's my mother-in-law takes care of him, because my wife, you can't count on her. No, Captain, no, of course not, I'm not abandoning him. It's my kid seeing as how he's my wife's kid, that is, my wife Marthe, but it's not my own personal kid. That is, it's a kid who didn't come from me, I mean. Between me and her, Marthe, everything had been over for a long time by the time the kid came along. But he's my kid all the same because that's how it is in the law. To figure out whose he is exactly, well, you'd have to know a thing or two. Nobody showed up to claim him, naturally. A kid who's in line to be a ward of the state. Ain't no luck on his side either.

And now, ladies and gentlemen, with this little all-purpose can opener that I've got here in my hand, I'm going to open a tin of sardines.

—HENRY MILLER

No luck on his side? *"Pas de pot?"*

Madame Bourladou appeared not to understand. I explained to her that it was a term existentialist philosophers use to define certain aspects of our situation in the world.

"Don't make fun of me, you're being stupid," Madame Bourladou had said, with a sugary-sweet smile.

Bourladou had just poured more armagnac in my glass for the third time. Back again in his chair, he sat with his thighs wide-flung, puffing, gleaming like a polished armoire.

"Tell me the truth, how do you find it?"

"How do I find it?"

"The armagnac, yes. You didn't notice you were drinking armagnac?"

I declared emphatically that the armagnac was great.

"One of my customers gets it for me. At truly bargain prices."

Bourladou doesn't mind occasionally treating me as a connoisseur. Earlier, while we were at table, he had solicited my opinion on the wine he got from someone in Touraine. I had sung its praises.

The truth is that about the only sort of wine I really appreciate is plain old lower-class red with its taste of iron and ink, the stuff my Company Five buddies and I used to swig. The truth is also that as concerns roast leg of lamb, I prefer it well done, dry, cooked almost black.

"You like it rare, don't you?" Madame Bourladou asked me.

Hardly a question: she had no doubt that I like it rare—that's how you have to like it. Didn't dare protest, I felt myself in the wrong. I sat back while a first and then a second amount of this flaccid pink matter was placed upon my plate. Bourladou's face, from cheekbones to chin, has that exact same color. (Madame Bourladou likes it rare.)

They invite me about once every six months: that's sufficient.

"Come and have dinner with us, it'll get your mind off things," Bourladou says bigheartedly.

He imagines his armagnac, his armchairs, and his conversation to have a beneficial effect on my mental hygiene. Get my mind off things? What does Bourladou know about the things my mind are on?

An entire evening to be spent in the odor of vanilla and cigars that one breathes in the homes of Good People. Showing an interest, or pretending to, in politics and in belles lettres.

On evenings such as these I put on the least crumpled of my ties, the gray one with the red stripes. I buy some flowers for Madame Bourladou from the old woman in front of the theater. A procedure which, I imagine, forms a part of my role as a guest. Madame Bourladou seizes hold of the bouquet with exclamations of wonder and almond-paste smiles.

"So very nice. But such extravagance. But you shall end up spoiling me . . . Solange, you'll put them in the Chinese vase . . . Do be careful, Solange, pay attention."

One hundred fifty francs worth of carnations. In return, I'm allowed oysters and leg of lamb, with wine from Touraine and wine from Burgundy. I come out ahead once again.

Jacques, across from me, is vigorously packing it in. Jacques is, for the moment, a scrawny kid with large paws and big knees. But you needn't worry: he will fill out, he will take on volume, thickness, weight, majesty, lard, and innards. He'll make them a real Bourladou. The species is not about to expire, the succession is assured.

I asked how this child's studies were progressing. It seems that his professors are satisfied with him, except in Latin, but he is being coached.

"Latin . . . ," Bourladou murmurs, with a touch of irony.

Jacques will be, like him, a man of action. One of those hefty chaps with broad asses. A useful and devoted citizen. A member.

"He has an intelligence quotient of one hundred and twenty," his mother confides to me.

"One hundred and twenty?"

"You haven't heard about this?" Bourladou says. "It's these things they've got these days in schools for finding out whether the pupils are intelligent. Like a thermometer, if you like."

"*Tests*," says Madame Bourladou, pronouncing that foreign word with care. "What they call 'tests.' I read a very thoroughly documented study on the subject in *Sélection*. They have you look at inkblots."

"And I got a hundred and twenty," the boy says.

"Yes," says his father. "Something the Americans have invented. It's curious that you haven't heard about it."

(My God, all these things they invent. The human race never ceases bringing itself to perfection. Television, ballpoint pens, zippers, tests, intelligence quotients . . .)

"There was this old guy that came into our classroom," says the boy, "with a beard and he smelled bad."

"Jacques, really," goes Madame Bourladou.

"Tell us a little about that," says the father.

The boy, his mouth full of leg of lamb, recounts that the bearded man had him repeat figures. And then that he gave him a sheet of paper on which there were little squares with tails.

"What were they for?"

"Had to cross some out," the kid says. "A real gas."

"Do they teach you those expressions at the lycée?" Madame Bourladou sternly inquires.

"The guy with the beard also came on with this about a

sergeant and a sparrow and a cow," the boy said. "Something like that, don't remember exactly. And then it came to one hundred and twenty for me. I was really pretty good with the letters part especially."

"What letters? Were you at least to make an effort to express yourself clearly . . ."

"It's sort of dumb. These letters they give you. And then you have to find the word. Letters jumbled up any old way. It was *I* and a *D* and *A* and *E*, the guy with the beard's letters. I saw it right away."

"It's the word 'ideal,'" I ventured.

"Four letters," Jacques replies, "not five."

We were rather anxiously hunting for the solution when from the kitchen there came an alarming sound of broken porcelain.

"Dear God . . ."

Madame Bourladou moaned tragically. She had brought one hand to that place upon her dress beneath which, approximately, the heart ought to be.

Solange appeared.

"Madame, it's the savarin," Solange said.

This avowal's elliptical form threw Bourladou into a sarcastic fury: "The savarin, the savarin . . . Plus the plate upon which you had placed it, I suppose. Well, my little one, you have my congratulations."

"My green and gold platter," Madame Bourladou was whimpering, "a plate that I was so fond of . . ."

Amputated of her pie plate, she was piteous to behold. Her crazed features expressed unfathomable distress. Solange waited, sly-faced, eyes downcast. A girl who was surely not unduly supplied with intelligence quotient.

"So this way, I guess, we'll be going without dessert," Jacques observed.

"A plate that we'd brought back from our honeymoon. We'd bought it in Florence . . ."

"In Venice," Bourladou rectifies. "Venice is where we bought it."

"No, darling, don't you remember, Venice was the desk lamp."

"Not a bit of it," Bourladou protests. "It comes from Padua, that lamp. If there is one thing I am sure of . . . But what the devil are you still doing in here? You think we haven't seen enough of you already?"

One imperial gesture, a "hmph, hmph," and Bourladou had whisked Solange's presence away.

"Back to the kitchen, my little one, go see what's left in there to break."

The incident cast a shadow over our evening together. Madame Bourladou arranged herself on the sofa, and for a long time gazed fixedly at the phantom of a pie plate. Bourladou talked to me about his cares as a public man, but listlessly. When I showed myself anxious to know whether the monument to the dead was not to be inaugurated soon, he appeared evasive and embittered.

All the planning has been done, however. The delegations, the music, the speeches. We can count upon the presence of a Danish diplomat and a colonel from the Horse Guards.

"In uniform?"

"Needless to say."

"No minister from the government?"

"Why, of course there will be a minister. How can you even imagine? . . . There's always a minister, there has to be . . . "

The name of the minister is not yet known, owing, Bourladou explained to me, to governmental instability. But it's not ministers we are short on, it's money.

"You have no idea how expensive one of these things can be."

All the more so since the initial project (the gymnastics instructor) has been periodically enriched by ornamental additions for which we are indebted to the ingenuity, to the devotion, and to the partisan passions of the Erection Committee's members. Each one of these initiatives has meant an increase in the overall bill. ("A substantial increase," in Bourladou's words.) Rave got all this started with his idea of a bronze plaque for the Names. The committee was unable to refuse him his plaque, but, soon afterward, Troude, at the urging of his friends, demanded that a wrought-iron grille extend around the symbolic athlete.

"It was a maneuver on the part of the minority, you understand."

The majority's reply to the grille was to require that the approach to the monument be by way of ornamental pylons. And thus, as if in the grip of some fever, in successive meetings the committee multiplied slabs and borders, cubes of granite and spheres of brass.

"It's demagoguery," Bourladou esteems. "We'll never manage to pay for all that."

For, although the monument may be proliferating in the brains of the committee, it's far from manifesting such exuberant vitality on what Bourladou calls the plane of concrete achievements. And the subscribers are not so numerous as had been hoped. And, Bourladou says, "You must see what these contributions are. One hundred francs, my friend. Fellows who are making money hand over fist, guys like Corchetuile, like Scie, they send you one hundred francs for a monument that'll run into the millions. Well, I'm sorry, I find that hard to take. You dedicate yourself, you bust your tail, you wheel and you deal, and some self-centered people, people who didn't take any risks during the war, who stayed home in their slippers, they shell out a one-hundred-franc bill. What the hell can you do with one hundred francs? Your employer, for instance, a gentleman who treats himself to American cars . . . "

"You're exaggerating," I said.

"What was that? Exaggerating?" Bourladou shouts. "A hundred francs, I swear. Not a centime more."

"I meant about the car. The boss drives a Simca."

"That's not the point," Bourladou snaps. "Don't mix things up all the time."

He concedes that the rumors which have been going around town for some time are hardly apt to revive the subscribers' zeal, and they will not help to turn the monument from nothingness into being.

"You're alluding to Widow Louchère?"

"Say," Bourladou exclaims in surprise, "how did you know?"

"Jacques dearest, it's your bedtime," Madame Bourladou decides briskly.

Jacques, who has been reading *Tarzan of the Apes* in a corner, objects that, darn it, it isn't even ten o'clock.

"Don't start acting like an imbecile," his father says.

Jacques, miffed, grunts some politesse, night mom, night dad, night sir, and to his exit imparts a surly, foot-dragging style.

We adults smile. We are musing on the comforting persistence of civic and human values.

"A drop of armagnac?"

Evenings such as these, cozy, seemly, are just what my father and mother used to hope for on my behalf, back when I was a young man. And not some little place in the evenings of other people, twice a year; rather, nothing but evenings like this one, evenings that were really mine, with the armchairs and the armagnac, with a child who would have an IQ of one twenty, with a spouse who would remind one of some soft piece of English pastry tricked out in paper lace . . .

"It's certain," Bourladou continues, "that Madame Louchère's conduct has not facilitated our task. You will tell me that in a sense she's acting no worse than many others . . . "

"Really though," Madame Bourladou protests, "two men at the same time, and men so much in the limelight . . . "

For there is no doubt whatsoever that Madame Louchère has become Chancerel's mistress, without having ceased however to be the mistress of Flouche. The town is watching to see how this situation develops. Some are indignant, others are chuckling, and the upshot of it is that this scandal is bringing discredit upon the committee over whose work Chancerel presides.

"It's annoying," Bourladou sighs, "very, very annoying."

"Athanase takes these things too much to heart," Madame Bourladou says.

In recent days I had indeed been noticing that allusions to Madame Louchère's private life were multiplying in the rue des Deux-Eglises urinal. I had noted, among others, this maxim by an anonymous moralist: "Two Resistance fighters are better than one." And this personal ad: "Deportee's widow, desiring to honor memory of her husband, seeks Resister, good situation, for sleeping partner." A charcoal drawing illustrates the foregoing inscriptions: two men and one woman, veilless. The artist, not interested in individual likenesses, had sought only to render, through a conventional amplification of some anatomical details, desire and voluptuousness. Not without felicity. It is a bit untruthful, but expressive and vigorous. And even possesses a troubling erotic vehemence. I found in it an echo of certain African figurines. Porcher, to whom I spoke about this, failed to see anything of interest in what I had to say. All four of his children have just come down with mumps, which has further soured my colleague's naturally peevish humor.

"Yes, well, they're going to tear down that *pissotière* of yours, you know. I have information."

"Tear it down?"

"And replace it with a new one, exactly. They've made up their minds at last. Between the two of us, it's about time."

I owned that it was about time. In my heart I deplored that this haven to naive art, independent opinion, and guilty passions might shortly disappear.

I questioned Bourladou about this measure. They were in absolute earnest, Bourladou confirmed. It had been adopted by the town council.

"But why are you asking me about that? Are you interested in urinals now?"

"I am interested in all that is human," I asserted.

Terence's words, or almost. Despite the classical dignity of this allusion, the conversation was bordering on vulgarity. I felt it urgent that it be got onto a more intellectual plane. Urgent to inquire, for example, about what Madame Bourladou was reading these days. To exchange a few formulas with her, such as:

No, I haven't read it, but they say it's very good.

Good lord, eight hundred pages, as many as that?

They're charging outrageous prices for books now. It wouldn't be so bad if they gave you your money's worth.

A real luxury, but you know how I am.

At least it's written in French and nowadays, you'll have to admit.

Between us, do you yourself believe in this *littérature engagée* they talk about?

That's right, André Rousseaux, in *Le Figaro littéraire*.

Etc.

And to wrap up:

"By the way, Athanase announced to me that you had finally chosen that terrific title you were looking for . . . "

"Well, actually . . . "

"And, can you imagine, he wasn't able to remember what it was."

"It's funny," Bourladou says. "Can you beat that? Tried my level best to think of it, but it had completely escaped me."

"It doesn't matter, you know."

"Yes, it does, it does," Madame Bourladou protests.

"You certainly understand, old man," Bourladou explains, "I've got so much on my mind, so many things in my head . . . "

I humbly contemplated that heavily laden head. Mine, by comparison . . . What is mine? A poor man's suitcase. Half empty. Nothing useful inside. Nothing but worn-out rags, threadbare clothes, old postcards, rusty cans, magazines from fifteen years back. You wonder why a person would hang on to all this rubbish, these preposterous leftovers. It's revolting. It does not have a pleasant smell.

"The only thing Athanase was able to recall was that you'd spoken about . . . let's see . . . "

"A symbol," Bourladou says.

"That's right," his wife says, "a symbol."

I have had enough. What in God's name am I doing in here with these two cretins? Enough of being the old friend who listens and answers and smiles. The old failure from Busson Brothers with his rumpled tie.

"So what was the title?"

A few syllables that were ringing in my brain: why this sudden reluctance to bring them out aloud—to utter them before these people? Yet this is not the first time that I have played this idiotic game.

"An idea, that's all . . . I haven't really made up my mind. An idea that occurred to me, while I was chatting . . . "

"Why, that is very interesting," declares Madame Bourladou.

A game? . . . I have the distinct feeling that it has finally taken a serious turn. That I desire (never have I felt this so strongly), that I desire now that this book exist, that it exist really, that it exist against Them and their bloody happiness.

"Yes, well . . . One evening, at the Trois Colonnes, the discussion having focused on Marécasse . . . "

"That poor Marécasse," Bourladou goes.

"A fellow who had no luck on his side," I say.

Those same words had for an instant caused the pathetic figure of Private Second Class Lebiche to stand there, among Madame Bourladou's marbles, bronzes, and Oriental vases. Again I saw his hands, hanging like dead animals. For an instant there were other unwonted presences there, cheek to jowl with the Valenciennes lace and the Venetian glass. Men with defeat on their faces. Those faces without names, those names without anything, those existences begot of the crowd and of chance, the fellows who have no luck on their side, the guys who are shoved ahead, who are dragged along, who are good for the road, good for the trains, I heard the sound of the wheels, good for the cattle cars, I heard the guys' voices, the clattering of the wheels upon the rails, the treading of so many feet upon so many roads, step after step, step after step, the sound of the wheels, the guys' snarling, worn, resigned voices, the voices of all the guys piled in there on top of each other and hauled around for nothing, because that's the way life is, because things are that way, because they have no luck on their side, no luck, no luck . . .

"No luck?"

Madame Bourladou lifted her plucked eyebrows a little to show that she was somewhat surprised and shocked by the expression.

Yes, I ought to get down to it. I've had enough of pretending to be writing a book. Really get down to it, once and for all. In the first place, I have hold of a title; that facilitates things. *The Cattle Car*—it's suggestive, it has a no-nonsense bluntness, the way they like their titles nowadays. I write the three words out in capital letters: *THE CATTLE CAR*. Truly not bad. A title that announces the difficult life, the hard knocks, the bitterness of the guy who has had a rough time. What the book has to do is show how we people are jammed into and lost inside the unintelligible, inside dark emptiness. Those who struggle and those who don't put up a fight. And those who explain where they are and where they are going, as if they knew, as if the situation their buddies were in didn't apply to them. (And they talk about the God of Mercy and Goodness, or about the Dialectics of History, depending upon where they did their studies.) The choice is up to me. My characters are only waiting for the signal to make their entrance. I give a cordial wink to the Unknown Soldier: you'll be in it, won't you now, old brother? And all those living creatures who are sound asleep within four walls, they, too, will be along on the trip. I go to the window. Familiar landscape: the wall, the sidewalk, the streetlamp, the poster. PUT YOUR CAPITAL TO WORK. It's true, am I not going to decide to put mine to work? By dint of existing, you cannot avoid accumulating some savings. The night is clear and dry. Out there three soldiers run past, with a great clatter of boots. Those of the next one. They are swearing thunderous goddamns because they're not going to make it back to the barracks in time. Boy oh boy, this time we're sure as hell in for it.

An evening like all other evenings. There are people snoring, people coupling, people unable to fall asleep because of their pain or their fear. "I see it again every single night," the Old Lady told me. "I'm helpless, it hits me deep inside my head." Once, long ago, her daughter threw herself into the canal. Bargemen rescued her. That's what's waiting for the Old Lady every night. "Until the day I die," she said, "I'll keep seeing that until the day I die."

"I'd left her how long? Five minutes. Not even five minutes. Couldn't I have seen it coming? Ah, it's something I'll never forgive myself for."

They had brought the mad girl back inert, wrapped inside blankets. Kids were following, ladies from the neighborhood who wanted to see. People came into the kitchen, giving their opinion, asking questions, arguing, getting their hands onto everything. After, there was mud all over the pavement outside. And the next day, it came out as a story in the newspapers, with the names, everything. That was the part that most humiliated the Old Lady.

"Just think," she goes on to tell, "she had to cross the whole of the lower town, with all those little streets so tangled up it's enough to get you lost twenty times over. We never once went that way with her. It didn't matter, she ran straight ahead, the people told me, like somebody who knows just where she's going. Well, you try and figure it out . . . "

A scene to use for *The Cattle Car*. An aspect of the suffering of living creatures buried in the opaqueness of existence, with their tenderness, their distress, their anger, their ridiculous goodwill, their heartrending helplessness. I know a few things about that. Things anybody at all can find out anywhere—on benches, in the straw of soldiers' temporary quarters, among the furnishings of furnished rooms . . . My education has been going on for a good forty years. Forty years: I ought to have ripened long ago, by now I should be a man who has been ripe for a long time. Odd expression: ripe. As for cheese. Fatty, soft, rotting, runny. I've not yet gotten to the point where I'm just right, but it shouldn't be long now. Not yet runny enough—an accommodating nature, agrees about everything, with everybody. It'll come; I, too, shall become habituated. But before attaining the perfection of human ripeness, before this unctuous maturity, this culminating, this completion, this rotting condition, I've got to try. I'm going to go back to my old jottings, my travel notes. Let me at least try to write *The Cattle Car*.

AFTERWORD

For Andrée Hyvernaud

Le Wagon à vaches was the second—and last—book that
Georges Hyvernaud published. When it appeared, in 1953, it
was coolly received by critics and the public alike; the edition did
not sell, and in due course it was pulped. Not until after his death
(on March 24, 1983) was Hyvernaud acclaimed a great writer following the publication of his *Oeuvres complètes*, issued between
1985 and 1987 in four volumes, the second of them being a reis-
sue of *Le Wagon*, with an enthusiastic preface by Etiemble. Afterward, in 1991, under the title *L'Ivrogne et l'Emmerdeur*, came a
volume of letters Hyvernaud addressed to his wife between
August 1939 and May 1940; and, also in 1991, adaptations of
his two books for the theater, which were staged by Jean-Louis
Benoît and successfully presented at the Théâtre de l'Aquarium
in Vincennes, then in several towns in the provinces. Finally, in
1995, *Feuilles volantes*, a collection of hitherto unpublished writings, appeared. And at last Hyvernaud received his place in dic-
tionaries of literature.

An author who while alive was ignored—except by a handful
of attentive readers—and who was extolled just after his death:
such was Hyvernaud's case, the opposite of that of those notori-
ous writers who as soon as they die sink into a twenty-year pur-
gatory of oblivion . . . Hyvernaud spent thirty years in his pur-
gatory without ever seeing its end. To the critics' disdain his
reply was silence, since he was to publish nothing after 1953,
apart from some manuals of literature for schoolchildren, of
which he was a co-author, and an essay on *Du côté de chez Swann*
in a pedagogical series. And yet, from 1926 until 1940, along-

side his teaching he had been active as a chronicler and literary critic, with articles published in various reviews.

Born near Angoulême (on February 22, 1902) into a family that was part peasant, part working class, Hyvernaud, after attending the normal school in Angoulême that trained teachers for the elementary grades, went on to the Ecole Normale Supérieure in Saint-Cloud (1922–24), after that becoming a professor of French in the normal schools at Arras (1925–34), at Rouen (1934–39), then, following the war, at Auteil (Paris). Before the war, he was politically on the left within the Front Populaire movement; close to the Communists, he joined the Association des Intellectuels antifascistes, wrote for *Monde*, Henri Barbusse's weekly, or for *Soutes*, a "revue de culture révolutionnaire internationale." (However, it was to *Les Primaires*, the monthly magazine for elementary-school teachers, that he gave the greater share of his articles.) But in 1938, considering his freedom of action and of expression jeopardized, and little disposed to play the part of *littérateur engagé* (or "*encagé*," according to the phrase in *Le Wagon à vaches*), he preferred to limit himself to the role of witness. Later, in 1947, when Simone de Beauvoir invited him to join the editorial committee of *Les Temps modernes*, he declined. "My independence means too much to me," he said. He nevertheless remained faithful to the convictions he had formed early on through contact with the common people and then fortified in the secular and progressive milieu of teachers.

Captivity (from May 1940 until April 1945) was to impart a different course to the writing he had begun to work at in 1926. He was now maintaining a diary, writing numerous letters to his wife, and filling notebooks with materials for a book on the life of the prisoners. That book, *La Peau et les Os*, completed at the end of 1947 (and of which a chapter, tentatively the first chapter, had been printed in the December 1946 issue of *Les*

Temps modernes), was brought out in March of 1949 by Les Editions du Scorpion.

Hyvernaud had already, in 1948, undertaken the composition of *Le Wagon à vaches;* at the end of 1950 he delivered it to the same publisher. But the latter, notwithstanding its commitments, put the manuscript away in a drawer; after equivocations, evasions, and lies, it decided not to publish it. Thanks to the interventions of friends, the book was issued by another publisher, Denoël, in May 1953. At that point Hyvernaud was well into a new novel, but he did not complete it. The vexations and humiliations connected with the publishing of *Le Wagon à vaches* had discouraged him. Add to that the critics' unfriendliness or silence, as well as his professional and family obligations. Around about 1954 or 1955 Hyvernaud gave up pursuing a writing career, whether as a novelist or a critic.

The only two books he published, and which ought to have come out in swift succession, are more closely related to one another than it seems at first glance. It may be pointed out that the opening chapter of *La Peau et les Os* (written and inserted at the last moment) presents, in the evocation of a family dinner following the Liberation, characters who greatly resemble the Habitués of the Trois Colonnes, the café in *Le Wagon à vaches.* More generally, the same ironic eye commands in both. While *Le Wagon* is an avowed "novel," its author declares (in the draft for a letter to one of his correspondents, in 1949) that in *La Peau et les Os* he has "tried to write a novelized essay," specifying that "my characters are fictitious—for the most part . . . I believe that the full expression of reality is to be achieved only by borrowing certain techniques from the novel." One has no trouble discerning, in the variety of tones and registers, the same novelistic procedures at work in both books. Let us add that certain characters—Ure, Chauvin, Vignoche—who appear fleetingly in *Le Wagon* as the narrator's fellow captives are familiar to the reader of *La Peau et les Os*. Barbeterre, whom the Habitués poke fun at, was glimpsed, at the café, before the war, as a soccer fan in the earlier narrative; Professor Dardillot of *Le Wagon* is undoubtedly the same as Dardillon, the narrator's colleague in the final chapter of *La Peau et les Os;* and so on.

The two books have, in part, a common matrix: the fragmentary manuscript that Hyvernaud produced between 1942 and November 1944 under the title *Voie de garage*, the first adumbration of *La Peau et les Os*. From it Hyvernaud also drew, for *Le Wagon*, essentially all of the chapter on the Habitués (save the passages concerning Marécasse). One notes, finally, that the narrator of *Le Wagon*, like the narrator of *La Peau et les Os*, underwent detention in Pomerania.

The author himself was at pains to indicate the second book's consanguinity with the first in the *prière d'insérer* copy for *Le Wagon:* "In his first book, Georges Hyvernaud described the condition of the prisoner of war. *Le Wagon à vaches* may be defined as the diary of a postwar prisoner, a commonplace kind of man locked inside his petty clerk's job, inside mediocre company and banal memories, captive of his town. Incomprehensible." That is, the novel proceeds, like the earlier narrative, from one and the same experience. It is its sequel and consequence. In 1949 or 1950 Hyvernaud underscored this continuity in an unfinished letter to Raymond Guérin, who contributed a preface to *La Peau et les Os:* "Captivity was not a lovely adventure. When I came back from it, the scene around me seemed generally to be one of jingoism and starry-eyed excitement, which produced in me a keen feeling of my own mediocrity. Only I was weak and spiritless. Looking more closely at all that, I suspected some charlatanism in those debauches of energy and glowing sentiments. I kept still. I did not have the floor. I didn't cut much of a figure, let me tell you." It's as though we were listening to the narrator of *Le Wagon!*

Nevertheless, this does not signify that the work is autobiographical. Earlier, apropos of *La Peau et les Os*, Hyvernaud was observing that "the narrator is not exactly the author." "It is to be hoped that this book will not be looked upon as an autobiography," Hyvernaud wrote in the *prière d'insérer* for *Le Wagon*. "If this book is cast in the first person, the reason for it is modesty. *I* is the most impenetrable of all masks." *I* is for him "the most mysterious pronoun of the lot." In *La Peau et les Os*, the narrator may be identified with the author—sometimes more, sometimes less—there being several *I*'s: a somewhat removed *I* in the family scene at the beginning; a very close *I* in the chapter on Péguy—but one that does not exhaust all that the author thought about that writer; a more personal *I* in "Our Noble Profession." In *Le Wagon* the distance widens between the author and the narrator, an employee at "Busson Brothers, Sparkling Waters." However, in what is said regarding literature, the *I*, in the main, expresses the opinion of the author. The entire novel is shot through with Hyvernaud's personal experiences, both remembrances and stories others told him. The provincial city, unnamed, is reconstructed from places the novelist had known: Angoulême, Rouen, and especially Arras. In the career and the person of the parliamentarian Flouche one may detect a resemblance to those of Guy Mollet, a star in Fourth Republic political life. One will observe, among other details, that the rue Désiré-Lemesle is a composite of the first name of a socialist mayor of Arras and the last name of his conservative predecessor. But why accumulate identifications of this sort? The work is not a roman à clef. This transposition aims at the typical and the symbolic. "A man like Flouche belongs to History and to the Masses." Like any other politician who "has made his way."

Actually, the novelist's intention is to bring out the underlying conditions of life during that revealing period when the Liberation brought passions and impostures to light as, in another manner, captivity had done. But here the subject broadens, inasmuch as, unlike prisoners in a camp, the community evolves within its normal framework. It is not just a question of recreating, with humor, the life of a society at a given moment, by means of a gallery of portraits in which Croquedale the restaurant keeper, Corchetuile the butcher, Canon Coudérouille, the bookseller Rudognon, and others seem to come from the world of Rabelais. What we have here is less a colorful rendering of provincial life than an examination of humanity—a humanity very close to animality (Bourladou in undershorts is "a monstrous fowl"; one of the Habitués is dubbed "the Batracian"; the crowd at a ceremony watches the movements of the government minister "as at the zoo it does those of the seals or the hippopotamus"). In short, men in a cattle car are just where they belong.

In reducing man to what is animal in him, the author is intent upon showing the metamorphosis brought about by social and cultural life, by an entire ensemble of artifices and stereotypes, whether these be the suit that makes Bourladou's belly "inspire the same respect as the safe deposit vaults and the facades of banks" or the outer clothing the customers get into when they leave the café; conversely, bedtime undressing is "the moment when humankind . . . renounces the coherent appearances it assumes for sixteen hours a day." At "this moment of truth," "only the backs of chairs are wearing jackets. And only jackets are wearing decorations."

One might say, echoing the famous Sartrean distinction, that the characters here have given up being persons: man no longer sees himself otherwise than before the eyes of another. However, the inner and ironic gaze of the narrator remains. That anonymous narrator, in his social situation, his mode of life, his physical appearance, his associations, his memories, etc., is the exact antithesis of his interlocutor, the central character, Bourladou—whose name had been given to the author by a mispronunciation on the part of one of his students who meant to talk about Bourdaloue (1632–1704), a Jesuit, one of the great consecrated orators of the court of Louis XIV, whose preachings were stamped with moral severity . . . To employ the phrase in Hyvernaud's *prière d'insérer*, Bourladou is "the man of comforts and conformisms." Through him—and his spouse—the satire attacks the world of illusions and of pretenses in which "Good People" give each other a good conscience, with Literature playing a role analogous to the one played by monuments to the dead.

Adjoining this sarcastic tableau, as a counterpoint to it, flows a compassion for common folk, for the humble who in their repetitious tasks are doomed to their "insect's destiny," people like Iseult next door, the Porcher family, the Old Man, the Old Lady, and their daughter, people like the keeper of the public garden and the little old men sitting on the benches there; a compassion for the victims of authority, such as the alleged Nazis terrorized by the M.P., or Private Lebiche; for the victims of ill luck, such as Bourladou's father or Uncle Ulysse; or again for the victims of ignominy, such as Marécasse. For all of those, the rights of man seem laughable indeed: Hyvernaud's original title for his as yet unfinished novel was *Les Droits de l'homme*. And as an epigraph, one of its chapters has a passage from Article II of the Déclaration des Droits of 1789. These rights, flouted in the war—as the chapter shows—become illusory with the return of peace ("Put your capital to work") and have little meaning for those who, like the narrator, mark time within the swarming mass of Crabs.

It has been advanced that this outlook, apparently pessimistic, resulted from the crucial experience of wartime captivity. Promiscuous incarceration among men completely gone to seed because of confinement and destitution would have inspired the writer, would have provoked this search for a human truth on the farther side of all idealizing preconceptions. This is to have failed to recognize a sensibility that impregnates most of the writings Hyvernaud published before the war. As early as 1927, in an article on the crosses in a military cemetery (from the First World War), he sees in these crosses "the sign of addition," of "an immense addition. Addition of sufferings, addition of corpses." And this "sign," by virtue of what it symbolizes, "delivers [one] from the rhetoric and the poetry by which war and peace are customarily defended." In 1928, in a piece on Charlie Chaplin, he observes that "our brother Charlot" is "the eternal pilgrim pursuing his pilgrim's course upon all the roads of distress" and who succeeds "within an absurd and unfeeling universe" in "maintaining his poor life surrounded by the malice of men and the pitfalls of fate. And wit ye well: that victory is a victory of the Spirit." One could also cite the 1935 portrait of Georges Duhamel as a "dealer in words," the fashionable lecturer who comforts the "provincial bourgeoisie," who "aids them not to see themselves as they are," in fine, the man who meets the expectations of all the Bourladous. And those are but a few examples.

If the experience of captivity had been decisive for the birth of the writer, the change it brought about was not in his point of view about man but about the act of writing. Until then Hyvernaud had written nothing except articles, most often upon recently published books. Now it is he who is going to write a book, then a second one. The ordeal of captivity had freed the writer that existed in him virtually. Those circumstances also toughened his vision. May one upon that account speak, as critics have tended to do, of pessimism, of nihilism, nay, of nastiness?

Hyvernaud noted with regard to Charlot that he assured "a victory of the Spirit" and incarnated "Intelligence" in the "hostile" and "absurd" world that surrounds men. *Le Wagon* illustrates this statement. Derision, withering irony, critical distancing with regard to false values mark the refusal of fakeries and impostures, and incite the reader to exercise his freedom himself, to master the event by himself giving it a meaning. Again with regard to Charlot: "It is a victory just to remain a man in the midst of brutes." That implies a "faith in man," as is admirably attested by the "Letter to a Little Girl," sketched in February 1945, during the harrowing exodus of the prisoners, and which was the first text Hyvernaud published after his return from having been a prisoner of war.

To keep the mind on the alert against all dulling and against all heroic travesty means not to be the dupe of appearances or clichés, hence to wring the neck of literature, to enforce a direct contact between writing and reality. That's where Hyvernaud's style gets its strength. His novel lacks a plot, but an ending is prepared for from the outset: as happens in the form inaugurated by *The Counterfeiters*, one watches the coming into being of the novel which will have as its title . . . *Le Wagon à vaches*. But this sly wink also advises us of what sets Hyvernaud apart from the idea Gide had of the novel and of literature. Here everything, all the way to the resources of caricature, is brought into play in order to prize off the social and cultural veneer overlaying original nudity, in order to signify the truth about persons and things. The narrator of *Le Wagon* says that in setting words "seriously, carefully" next to words, he is seeking the shortest path from the opening point of the sentence to the semicolon. Hyvernaud also is finding the shortest path from the word to the real, with "these little sentences which proscribe big words" (Etiemble).

Is it surprising that Hyvernaud's merits went unrecognized at the beginning of the 1950s? It does indeed seem that he was given only a superficial reading then. At a time when France was emerging haloed from the victory won with the Allies against Nazism, it was not appropriate to present a cheerless and murky picture of the French—those of them who had been held captive and those of the Liberation; it did not fit in with the ambient patriotism. This writer, if I may use the expression, was not politically correct. Has he now become so? Without doubt, times have changed, and Hyvernaud's success in the 1980s coincides with another perception of the Occupation, with, to be precise, a new insistence upon the truth—above all on the part of the younger generations—concerning a cloudy and complex moment in French history; with, too, a renewed attentiveness to the freer forms of writing by which literature is called into question. And so it is understandable that the writer be appreciated today. But if one pays attention to the novelist's stringent humanism, to the acuity of observation that is without mercy for any conformism, present or to come, and that makes of him, in Etiemble's words, "an individual on the alert," Hyvernaud is not and shall never be politically correct.

Roland Desné